WOLF

ANNALEE ADAMS

WOLF

First edition. May 2024.

Copyright © 2024 Annalee Adams.
The moral rights of the author have been asserted.

Written by Annalee Adams.
This is a work of fiction. Similarities to real people, places, or events are entirely coincidental.
All rights reserved.

No part of this publication may be reproduced, transmitted or stored in a retrieval system in any form or by any other means, without prior written permission from the author, Annalee Adams. No part of this publication may be circulated in any form of binding or cover other than that in which it is published.

ISBN: 9798324214302

This book has been typeset in Garamond.
www.AnnaleeAdams.biz

All suffering originates from craving, from attachment, from desire.

Edgar Allen Poe

ANNALEE ADAMS - WOLF

1

The bloated man groaned, grinding up and down on top of me. Reality was never a place I longed to live anymore. His whiskey breath, and the sweat dripping from his forehead, made me want to die inside every time he touched me. The only way I survived these encounters was to disappear. To remember, I am not my body, and my body is not me.

Forgotten figures silhouetted my mind as the memory of my parents blessed me once again. My mind escaped, travelling back to a place of happiness, of the last smile I ever gave, the final laugh I ever heard. Before it all started, one evening at the young age of thirteen.

I perched on the old wooden swing hanging from the ancient oak in our backyard, my feet dragging through the wild grass beneath. A breeze teased through my red hair, coaxing it into a fiery dance against the pallor of my skin.

"Evie!" My mother's voice yelled out from the kitchen window, warm and honeyed as she tended to her freshly baked apple pie. "Don't go too far, sweetie!"

I never planned to. The world beyond those familiar houses and friendly trees was nothing but a shadowy tale to me. I rolled my eyes. If only I knew the truth beyond my backyard.

The day unfolded like every other. The morning was spent reading and creating tall tales as I stared out at the dancing shapes in the clouds from my bedroom window, and the afternoon humming tunes while I helped Dad in the garden;

his laughter rich and echoing against the silent whispers in the garden.

My past life seemed like a dream, a memory I longed for with every fibre of my being. It was a symphony of familiarity, soothing like the lullabies my parents sang to chase the nightmares away. The world was predictable and comforting, from the friendly greetings of neighbours to the expected clatter of the postman's footsteps. I was sheltered in its mundane normalcy, cocooned in the warmth of a family whose love ran as deep as the roots of the towering oak tree I used to swing from.

My innocence was once pure and untainted. Happiness used to be so easily within reach, but what once was, now feels like a temporary illusion.

I had everything and more, or so I thought. Maybe that was the problem. Maybe I was given too much love and laughter too soon, and now I'm paying the price for it.

As I lie here on this bed, with its pristine white ceiling and creaking bedposts, I can't help but think that this is all my fault. If only I had been smarter, stronger, braver... maybe I could have prevented this nightmare from happening.

But no amount of beating myself up would change the fact that I was trapped under this vile old man, feeling his hands over me and his body crushing mine. His cigar-stained teeth and alcoholic breath make me want to crawl out of my body.

At thirteen years old, I never imagined this darkness could exist, and now it's all I know. It makes me hate my skin, wishing I could rip it off and start anew. But even if I did, the scars would remain, both physical and emotional. And at the end of the day, I am still stuck here, living in a world where monsters like him exist and little girls like me are their prey.

I remember my final evening with my parents, my heart beating in time with the quiet of our home, blissfully unaware of the shadows creeping closer to the edges of my sunlit world.

I had a soft spot for story time, and yes, I may have been too old, but I loved the way my mother wove the words into a magical rhythmic tune, changing even a basic fairy tale into a fully-fledged fantasy over the space of a few nights.

This evening, it was Red Riding Hood, one of my favourites.

As I changed for bed, I stared out of my old wooden window, gazing past the oak tree that stood tall and proud in our garden.

But tonight, as I changed for bed, something caught my attention beyond the tree. Far down the path, illuminated by the streetlights, were three figures standing in a row. They seemed to be staring up at me, their eyes piercing into mine even from this distance. I gulped.

My heart began to race and a chill ran down my spine. What were they staring at? I looked behind me. Nothing unusual, just my old bedroom. Then I looked back and they were gone. I searched left to right, eyes narrowed, brow furrowed. But there was no sign of anyone there.

"Ready?" My mum said, walking in, making me jump out of my skin.

Her eyes widened. "Everything okay?"

I nodded. "Mmhmm. I thought I saw something."

"Oh, it's probably a cat. We seem to be getting quite a few strays around here recently."

"Mmm, probably," I replied, still staring out of the window.

"Come on then," Mum said, patting the bed.

I took a long deep breath, closed the curtains and jumped into bed, snuggling under the duvet and blankets.

"So, tonight my Evie, I will tell you the tale of a girl I know, called Red," she smiled.

"Red began her life just as any little girl would, full of hopes and dreams. With the unconditional love of her mother, the adoration of her father and the unwavering support of her grandmother, Red felt invincible."

I nodded, smiling.

"One day, as her father chopped wood for the fire, Red eagerly promised to bring a loaf of freshly baked bread to her grandmother who lived deep in the woods."

"Donning her signature red hooded coat and gathering a basket filled with warm bread and cheese, Red set off on the familiar path to her grandmother's house."

"She had travelled this path countless times before, accompanying her father on wood-gathering trips and even fending off dangerous predators."

"But on this particular day, something felt different. An eerie feeling crept into Red's bones as she walked deeper into the dense forest." I nodded.

"She pushed the feeling back, picked up her pace and sang a little song to herself as she skipped along. The next thing…"

That's when everything changed, as there was a knock at the door downstairs. Mum stopped and shrugged, letting my father get the door. She continued the story.

"The next thing she heard was a monstrous snarl echoing through the trees, freezing Red in her tracks. She could hear branches snapping and leaves rustling as whatever lurked in the shadows drew closer."

My eyes widened and she smirked. "Mum! I'm not going to sleep after this!" She laughed, continuing.

"Fear paralysed little Red as she realised that she might not make it out of those woods alive." I bit my lip, pulling the blanket up to my chin. "She ran as fast as she could to her grandmother's house, hearing the thudding sounds of not one, not two, but three hairy wolves chasing her." I gasped.

"Just as she was about to give up hope, a deep, gravelly voice called out from beyond."

Downstairs the door slammed and something broke. Mum's eyes narrowed and I sat upright, my heart pounding. "Wait here sweetie," she said. I'll be back in a minute. It's probably your father tripping over his walking stick again!" I nodded laughing nervously as she left.

Snuggling down into the duvet, I took a few deep breaths calming myself down, thinking about how little Red could get away while trying not to fall asleep before I heard the end of the story.

The next thing I knew, I was startled awake by the sound of my mum's screams. I froze, my heart hammering in my chest.

"MUM!" I yelled, jumping out of bed. I was halfway out of my room when I noticed him for the first time, Edison, one of the Payne brothers.

He leant against the bannister rail fidgeting with a lighter, almost as though he was waiting for me all along. I stopped dead in my tracks.

His sudden appearance was a crack in the glass of my menagerie, an intrusion upon the peace.

I'd heard whispers of the brothers, dark murmurs that had spread through the town like wayward spirits. These were men who thrived on debts owed and promises broken, collectors of dues in the most harrowing sense.

My father's voice echoed in my head—a conversation muffled by walls, but clear enough to chill my blood. Debts. Money. Danger. The Payne brothers' names had been entwined with dread, a triad of omens that had no place in our tranquil existence.

A chill skittered across my skin. It wasn't only a shiver from the cool air of an open window; it was the prickle of his eyes boring into me. The malice that clung to him bellowed out like an aura—a knot formed in my stomach, heavy and foreboding. Dad's whispered confessions of debt and fear echoed in my ears, a melody of desperation that now made sense.

Edison's eyes meet mine—an unwelcome connection that felt like a nail driven into the coffin of my hope.

"Evening, Evie," he drawled, his voice a deep rumble that vibrated through the hallway.

"Leave me alone," I said, my voice barely above a whisper.

I tried to run past him, but in an instant, he darted forward, closing his hand around my arm with a vice-like grip. "Not so fast little one. We need to have a chat about your father's promises."

"Let me go!" I shouted, panic slicing through my veins as I tried to wrench free, but his grasp only tightened, his fingers branding my flesh.

Downstairs I heard my mother yelling for me to run. But there was no chance. I pulled and tugged at him, kicked and punched, there was no getting free. He laughed. "Every time you hurt me, I will hurt you much worse later on," he promised. I gulped.

"You leave her alone!" my father's broken voice yelled from downstairs. That's the last words I heard him say. What followed was a loud thud, and my mother's tragic screams as she burst into floods of tears.

"George NO!" she cried.

"DAD?" I yelled.

"He can't help you any more Evie. You belong to us now." My eyes widened; my jaw dropped. "Come quietly, and maybe we will spare your mother," he said, a threat cloaked in deceit.

My heart hammered against my ribs, every beat a drum roll to impending doom. The tranquil world I knew that morning was shattered; replaced by a nightmare with open eyes.

"SOMEONE HELP!" I screamed, the words ripping from my throat, but they drowned amongst the screams my mother was making downstairs.

"Behave, Evie, every time you misbehave it will cost you dearly." I burst into tears. "Oh, for fucks sake!" He wrapped his arm under me, threw me over his shoulder and took me downstairs.

As I left, all I saw was my father's battered body lying unconscious on the floor, and my mother weeping beside him.

***

"Stefan, Xander, you know what to do," Edison ordered as he took me outside, his brothers nodded and went in to finish the job.

Forcing me into the back seat of his car, he slammed the door shut, locking, and sealing me inside with him.

Moments later the back door opened next to me and Xander got in, wiping bloodied hands on his jeans. He grinned at me "Hey cutie!" he said, placing his hand on my thigh. I slapped it away and snarled at him. He laughed.

Stefan got in the driver's side, "All done, let's go."

Edison nod's and soon the world outside blurs into streaks of colour. But inside the car, the horror is crystal clear. My breath comes in jagged gasps as I strain against the seatbelt they've wrenched across my chest, binding me to this nightmare.

"Stop squirming," Stefan growled from the driver's seat, his eyes meeting mine in the rear-view mirror—cold, like cubes of ice.

I refuse to cower. "You can't just take people," I spit out, my voice fierce despite its tremble. The car's interior is a tomb; their silence is the stone sealing it shut.

Xander leaned over his face inches from mine. "We can do whatever we want," he replied, his tone laced with hateful calm. His breath smells of mint, a bizarre contrast to the malice in his gaze.

I kicked at the leather seats, ignoring the ache in my legs. The air was thick with the scent of their cologne, a mixture of pine and something darker, like the promise of decay. "My family will find me!" I declared, but my words were hollow, eaten by the void that these brothers seem to command.

"Family?" Edison chuckles darkly, twisting to face me. His eyes are the darkest of the three, abysses that threaten to pull me under. "Your father should have thought about family before debts were made."

Their laughter was a symphony of dread, notes that curled around my heart and squeezed. The car sped on, racing through the night like a vampire fleeing the dawn. These men, the Payne brothers, are the monsters of my nightmares come to life. And as they took me away from everything I know and love, I clung to my determination like a shield. It was all I had left in the abyss.

***

The next thing I remember is being jolted awake by the sound of a car door slamming shut. My heart hammered against my ribs, and I tried to move, but my hands were bound, and I was trapped. Panic clawed at my throat as I realised, I was no longer in the car.

"Get up," Stefan's voice was like a whip, cracking through the air. "You're coming with me."

"Where are we?" My voice trembled, and I hated myself for it. I should be stronger than this.

"Somewhere safe," he says, his words dripping with malice. "For us, not for you."

I didn't know what to say, or how to react. All I could do was stare at him, willing him to give me an answer.

"Your father owed us a lot of money," he continues, his eyes narrowing. "And you're going to help us get it back."

My stomach sank, and I felt sick. My mind reeling with questions, doubts, and fears. How much does my father owe them? Why would they take me? What do they want from me?

"Please," I whisper, tears stinging my eyes. "Let me go. I won't tell anyone."

"Shut up," Stefan said, spitting the words out, his disgust clear. "You don't get to talk anymore."

I tried to fight back the tears, but they came anyway, rolling down my cheeks like tiny rivers of despair. This can't be happening. It can't be. But deep down, I knew it was real, and I was trapped in a nightmare that I would never wake up from.

"Make no mistake, Evie," Edison murmured, his breath a ghostly whisper against my ear. "You belong to us now."

As we entered the mansion, the grandeur of the foyer did nothing to ease the knot of dread in my stomach. Marble floors reflected twisted shadows that danced with my every step. Photos lined the walls of young girls in pretty pink dresses and smiles as fragile as porcelain, their eyes following me, witnesses to my imprisonment.

My room was like a cell dressed in velvet and lace. The bed was large and uninviting, shrouded in darkness. Stefan locked the door from the outside, the sound echoing like a gunshot in the stillness of the night. "You will stay here tonight," he said, slamming the door as he left.

I sunk to the floor, the chill of the marble leeching into my bones. Hugging my knees, I stared into the void of my new existence. The silence was oppressive, punctuated only by the distant howl of the wind.

In this grand house of horrors, every creak and whisper of the ancient structure was a reminder of my vulnerability. The shadows seemed to creep closer, eager to claim me as one of their own. As the last light of day faded from the horizon, I was left with the bitter taste of foreboding and the certainty that my life had taken a dark and dangerous turn.

The bedposts stopped moving, and the man stiffened and groaned heavily. I could feel myself cringing and recoiling from his touch. He disgusted me. They all did. He eased himself up off the bed, grinning, throwing my nightdress at me. I didn't look at him, instead, I waited for him to leave, so I could shower in the hottest water I could manage and sit and scrub myself red raw.

Every time it happened, I would sit under the droplets of burning water, allowing myself five minutes to let go, five minutes to cry and say why me?

But after that, I had to be silent. Strong. Resilient. For if I wasn't, I would end up like them. The girls that disappeared; and the only way I would survive this hellhole is to play their game until I found a way out… then kill every last fucking one of them.

2

The following night my body was tied up and forced again. The white ceiling moved back and forth, bedposts creaked and groaned and I disappeared into what happened after I was taken.

I never had a chance to wake peacefully in the room of velvet and lace. Instead, my heart pounded in my chest as I was dragged down the bed, and yanked out of sleep kicking and screaming.

Edison's shadow loomed over me, a dark cloud ready to burst. His smile was sinister, his eyes two pools of malice that sought to drown me in dread.

"Morning, Evie," he purred, his voice laced with a threat that slithered through the air like venomous smoke.

I couldn't move, couldn't breathe; my heart hammered against my ribcage, begging for escape. But there was nowhere to flee. The room of luxury disappeared behind me as he dragged me from it, parading me down the corridor, his intention as clear as the glint of his knife in the morning light.

The hallway was a blur of shadows and whispers, the scent of decay growing stronger with every step we took. My heart slammed against my ribs, each beat a deafening drum in the oppressive silence.

Kicking open another door, he hauls me inside and I fell to the floor, the door slamming shut behind us. The room was a chilling tableau of horror. Studio lights blazed harshly, casting stark illumination over items that belonged in nightmares, not reality—an axe that gleamed with a sickly sheen, bondage gear that spoke of unspeakable pain, a one-way mirror for onlookers, and plastic sheets draped over what once might have been an ordinary bed.

As I turned I saw the giant above me—Edison Payne, looming in the doorway like the harbinger of doom. His eyes find mine, I can't breathe; I can't think. There's only the primal urge to escape, but my limbs betray me, rooted to the spot I fell upon.

"Evie," he says, my name curling off his tongue like poison. Before I can even attempt to run, his hand encircles my arm, his grip iron as he yanks me upright and I stagger forward.

And there, amidst the grotesque collection, a noose swings gently from the ceiling, its mere presence a scream in the silence. I shiver, feeling the ghostly touch of it against my skin, a macabre promise of potential ends.

"Beautiful, isn't it?" Edison's voice slides

over the scene, his satisfaction palpable. His breath is hot against my ear, and I flinch away, repulsed by his proximity. I look around desperately, seeking any flaw in this chamber of horrors that might offer salvation. But there is none; every detail is meticulous, every item a testament to his control.

My life teeters on the edge of a knife, and I am acutely aware of the fragility of my existence. In this room, under these lights, with this man, I am nothing more than a pawn in a game too twisted for comprehension. Anguish coils tight in my chest, but I swallow it down. I will not give him the satisfaction of seeing my fear. Not now, not ever.

I lunge forward, my hands clawing at the air, aiming for Edison's cold eyes. He steps back, his lips curling into a sneer. "Fight all you want," he hisses, his voice coated with malice. "It only makes it more enjoyable when I snuff out your little flame."

My heart hammers against my ribcage, thudding with primal, raw fear. But beneath that terror lies a seething ember of rage. They think they can break me, but I am not so easily shattered. Memories of home, of my family's warm embraces, ignite a fury within me, and I refuse to let this be my end.

"Never," I spit out, my voice trembling as much with defiance as with fear. I charge at him like a wild creature, knowing full well that hesitation means death. My nails rake across his cheek, drawing a thin line of blood that trickles down his pallid skin.

Edison recoils, his face contorting in anger, but I don't stop. I kick, bite, and scream, pouring every ounce of desperation into each movement. His grip tightens on my wrists, and I feel the world constrict around me. Pain blossoms where his fingers dig into my flesh, and for a moment, everything blurs—my vision dims, my resolve wanes.

But then, from the shadows, salvation bursts forth—a figure clad in darkness, marked by a broken heart tattoo etched into the skin on his hand. The door crashes open, and the masked man charges with the ferocity of a storm. Edison's attention snaps to the intruder, giving me a split second of distraction.

"Get off her!" the man roars his voice a thunderclap that echoes through the room. He tackles Edison, pulling him away from me.

I collapse to the floor, my breath coming in ragged gasps. As I watch the struggle before me, my mind races. This could be my one opportunity to flee from this abyss. I can't waste it—I won't.

The masked man throws Edison to the floor, standing over him. "Have your fun boy, but this one, we're keeping," he says.

Edison growls, getting up and brushing himself off. "Yes, father."

My brow furrowed and the masked man walked over to me and offered me his hand to help me up from the floor. I take it and he lifts me into his arms. "You may call me Daddy, Babydoll." I stood stunned in silence.

The father walked out, leaving me alone with Edison who laughed, turned to face me and said, "Where were we then?"

***

That was when I was thirteen. Edison was the first, and since then I've lost count. I remember the confusion as it swirled within me, a stormy sea crashing against the rocks of fear and revulsion. Every fibre of my being had screamed to resist, but the more I pushed back, the more they enjoyed it. I wasn't going to give them the satisfaction of that.

That asshole violated me, shattering my innocence like fragile glass upon the unforgiving floor. Shame engulfed me for so long, a crimson tide staining my soul, leaving me fragmented. But then one day I realised I was not my body anymore. This skin did not define me. I may have been molested, hurt, raped and abused, but inside I could be whoever I wanted to be. Which is why I live a different reality when it happens. I don't always wander back into the memories. Sometimes I tell a tall tale, like my mother did, some fantastical rhythmic wonder that cures the more broken sickness around us.

It wasn't all bad. I'd be lying if I said it was. Granted if you could get over the stench of death and decay. The fear of not knowing if today was your last, then the house was pretty nice and the grounds were quite stunning, well… except for the electric fences and guard dogs.

My family though, my sisters-in-arms. I've grown to love them. We're going through the pain together, and the only way we get through is by sticking together and having each other's backs. They're my girls. I smiled faintly, which the hefty man on top of me mistook for pleasure and continued to rotate his hips boring me to death.

After Edison had his way with me he took

me to where I live now, mine and the girl's room. I still remember the door creaking ominously behind me as he pushed in there. My eyes widened in horror as I took in the sight of the other captive girls huddled together, their faces etched with fear and despair. They were all so young, ranging from what looked to be similar ages to me, to just a few years older. My heart broke for them, knowing that we were all trapped in this hellish nightmare together.

I tried to hold back tears, but I could feel them pricking at the corners of my eyes. I didn't want him to see me cry. I had to be strong, or else I'd never make it out of here alive.

The door slammed shut behind me, with a finality that echoed through my bones. My legs gave way, and I crumpled onto the cold, unyielding floor of the cramped room. A chorus of shallow breaths filled the space, each one laced with terror. The air was thick, almost tangible in its heaviness, clinging to my skin like a shroud.

I hugged my knees to my chest, my naked body trembling uncontrollably.

At the end of the room, three girls huddled together. A pair of eyes lock onto mine, Natasha. Even in the dim light, her gaze cut through the gloom, sharp and calculating. Her eyes, rimmed with the remnants of mascara, held stories of a hardened survivor. She'd seen the darkness that lurked within these walls and had survived its icy fingers clawing away at her soul.

She watched me, and her eyes narrowed. One of the girls, our Jess, said something to the others. "Stay strong," she mouthed to me, as she muttered something to the other girls. The words were barely a whisper, yet they resounded like thunder in my ears. It has been a mantra for those who've had their light dimmed, but refuse to let it extinguish.

I drew in a ragged breath, tasting the stale despair that hung in the air. My heart continued its relentless pounding, each beat a reminder of the nightmare I was living. Yet beneath the cacophony of fear, there was a quiet voice that refused to be silenced. It whispered of defiance, of a will that bends but does not break.

The hushed voices of the other girls seeped into my consciousness, a low murmur that ebbed and flowed with tales of terror. I pressed my back against the cold wall, trying to make sense of the fragmented whispers that filtered through the stale air like uncovered secrets. They speak of things no one should ever know, nightmares made flesh within these cursed walls.

"Remember Lila?" A voice quivered from the corner, shrouded in shadow. "She screamed for days... then silence." The words hang heavy, a chilling warning.

"Shh," Jess hissed, her eyes darting nervously toward the door.

I drew my knees to my chest, wrapping my arms around them tightly as if I could shield myself from their fate. My heart felt like a lead weight, each throb a painful reminder of our shared captivity. I closed my eyes, but the darkness behind my lids was no sanctuary; it was a canvas for the horrors that stalked my thoughts.

Even in my nightmares, I could never have imagined something so terrifying. I could still smell him on me, the stench of cigars on his stale breath, and alcohol seeping from his sweat-covered body. It crawled across my skin, like lice infesting all over me, burrowing down, nesting, laying eggs, billowing and bursting, waiting to hatch. I vomited again in the corner.

It was my first time. It should have been beautiful. Not held down and attacked by the monster that is Edison Payne. Every part of me ached, and bruises although they would heal on the outside, would remain forever etched in my soul. It was a memory that had changed me, stolen my innocence, and brought me bursting into the reality of the dark world we lived in.

"Come on," Jess said walking towards me.

"Let's get you cleaned up,"

I shuddered away from her, my arms wrapped around my knees, tears streaming down my face.

"If you're not cleaned up when he comes back, he will get angry," she warned. "I'm trying to help you." She held out her hand.

"Just leave her", the other girl said on the other side of the room. "She'll be gone in two days, just like Lila or even Sara, remember her?"

Gone? What does she mean by gone? What happened to the others? Am I just another number, another lost soul, taken and forgotten? Will I be sold as unwanted goods, past their sell-by date? Now he had taken my virtue, what was their left to sell?

I fixed my gaze on a crack in the floorboards, tracing its jagged path with my eyes. It's a small thing, inconsequential to anyone else, but to me, it became an anchor, a thin line separating me from the abyss that beckoned with each whimper, each shudder of a girl too young to face such monstrosities.

I scanned every inch of the room, my mind sharpening with the precision of a blade. The walls were lined with peeling wallpaper, and the heavy drapes that blocked any sliver of light from the outside world seemed impenetrable. Yet, I search for seams, for any hint of weakness in this prison. The others huddled in corners, but my eyes were drawn to the ceiling, where the plaster had crumbled, revealing the skeleton of the house.

"He likes to have the first try," the younger girl, Beth said, breaking the silence. "Just ignore Natasha, she's been here the longest, the most cynical." The mean girl snarled at her and she smirked. "She's been through some shit."

"Haven't we all," Natasha stated. She looked at me. "You won't last five minutes if you keep crying girl," she said. "You've got to woman up. Sort yourself out!"

"Sort myself out!" I said, wide-eyed.

"Yeah put your big girl pants on!" Natasha exclaimed.

I huffed and looked down. "I don't have any pants anymore," I said, defeated. "He took them."

She rolled her eyes, rummaged through a stack of clothes, looked over, rummaged again then threw me a nightdress. "They don't allow pants here."

"Wait!" the girl next to me said, taking the nightdress before I could touch it. "You're covered in god only knows what with what he did to you. Shower first!"

I looked down and I was covered in dried blood from the cuts he had strategically made with his knife, sweat from his vile body and semen as he ejaculated inside then all over me. I gagged and Jess grabbed the bin just in time.

"Shit girl," Natasha said. "That is nothing compared to some of the shit we've been through. If you want to survive, you have to toughen up. Switch off when it happens. Go somewhere else. That's what I do."

"Yeah. That's what we all do," Jess said.

"What do you mean?"

"I don't know. Make up a story in your head, or relive happy memories with your family, anything but this place." I nodded.

"Is it gonna happen again?" I asked, finally taking the tall girl Jess's hand.

She nodded. "I'm afraid so. What's your name?" she asked after they all introduced themselves.

"I'm Evie. Well welcome Evie. We've got each other's backs here. The only way you survive this is to be strong and be silent."

"Silent?" I asked as she showed me to the bathroom. "Yeah. They don't like crying, screaming or answering back. The girls that did that didn't last five minutes." Gulping I bit my lip.

"Here, now take a shower, maybe they'll give you a few days to settle in before anything else happens. My eyes widened and I stepped into the shower, fell to the ground and cried under the droplets, allowing myself five minutes.

That first meeting saved my skin that day. No crying, no screaming and no answering back. It's what's happened next that surprised me.

ANNALEE ADAMS - WOLF

3

The four of us had made it through several close calls. I know I'd been here almost three years by the time the next girl joined us. It was nice to no longer be the newbie anymore, but at the same time, I felt horrendous for the poor kid, seeing myself in her eyes. Eyes of fright, pain, misery and self-loathing. She had nothing left to live for, and her attitude to life was not one of survival, it was more one of annoyance; an annoyance at being alive. It wasn't long before the brothers grew tired of her. I guess by now they needed their fill of sickening fantasies that went too far.

The strangest thing about it was that we knew when they all came to collect her, what was going to happen. But she didn't look afraid. She didn't seem sick to the stomach or ready to run at the first chance she had. No, Laney Milano, our fourteen-year-old beauty from the South side, appeared to smile for the very first time since she came here. She appeared relieved. Did she want this? Had she been hopeful that one day they would dish up her death on a silver platter so she could come and take it? Maybe the alternative of living a life of violence and abuse was worse than dying. I guess in most people's eyes it would be. Heck, in mine it is, most days at least. The only thing that keeps me going is the seething desire to gut the brothers like the pigs they are. I wanted to have fun with them. I wanted to cut them up and watch them squirm. I took a long, deep breath, thinking about Laney Milano.

"What's up buttercup?" Beth said, sitting

herself next to me on my bed.

I smiled. "I was thinking about Laney."

"Yeah, she was weird!"

I nodded. "Just a bit!" I paused. "But, did you see her smile when they took her?"

"Yeah, I'd not seen her smile before. It kinda creeped me out."

"I know right!"

"Stop gossiping!" Natasha said, walking over.

"What, are you telling me Laney didn't creep you out?"

"Of course she did, but she didn't deserve whatever they did to her… you know that."

I sighed, lowering my head. She was right.

"So do you think they'll bring someone else in?" Jess asked, from her bed over the other side of the room.

"God, I hope not!" Beth said.

"I did overhear Xander say they'd let us outside soon."

"Wait! What?" I cried, perching on the edge of my bed. It felt like months since we'd been allowed outside. She nodded. I smiled. I missed the outdoors, it reminded me of the good times with my parents.

"Why?" Jess asked. "Why are they doing that?"

"Maybe because they killed one of us?" Beth replied.

I shuddered. "Could be," Jess shrugged.

A sudden creak outside the door sent a jolt through us all, like a current electrifying our senses. Whispers died on trembling lips as bodies moved in a frenzied ballet of fear. Natasha, Jess and Beth ducked behind tattered furniture, pressing themselves into shadows that offer scant concealment. I felt their terror, but it didn't seize me—it fueled me.

Footsteps grew louder, thudding against the old wood of the hallway, each one a countdown to our collective nightmare.

The footsteps halted, hovering just beyond the threshold of our hell. The handle turned with the screech of ungreased metal, and the door swung open, casting a sliver of light that sliced through the gloom.

Daddy. His eyes smiled, as the ski mask he wore moved over his face. "Babydoll, how kind of you to greet me," he said.

I feigned a smile in return. I had learnt to play this man at his own game. By being polite and respectful, it meant he looked out for me and the girls, protecting us from greater harm, should his sons feel it ever need come our way.

"This afternoon, you and your girls will be allowed to picnic in the gardens. Please enjoy the beautiful weather. You could do with a little sunshine on that pale skin of yours." He smiled again.

I nodded, smiling back.

"I will leave you be. Your morning is your own. Breakfast will arrive shortly."

"Thank you," I said as he left, closing the door behind him.

Eyes wide, I turned to the girls. We had the whole day to ourselves! I wasn't sure why, or what we had to do to earn this, but I was grateful nonetheless!

***

After being cooped up inside for what felt like an eternity, beyond those pristine clean walls and that sterile universe they called a mansion, I needed fresh air. This afternoon the Payne brothers had allowed us that. Call it for good behaviour. Today was about the beauty and the sunlight, as the warmth cascaded down, kissing my skin with its delicacy. The air was fresh and breathable again. No more suffocation, no more claustrophobic feelings in those rooms. Out here, we were free, albeit behind electric fences, guarded by guards and dogs with sharp canines.

Walking barefoot on the grass I felt the blades cushion beneath my toes, comforting me in all of the ways I needed and more. It reminded me of the summer evenings I spent with my mother and father, sitting beneath the old oak tree, listening to the birds sing and dance, watching their babies attempting to fly for the very first time. It was always a beautiful time of year.

On a day like today, I would have been out planting vegetables with my father, or digging up potatoes ready for dinner. My mother, on the other hand, loved to bake, which suited my father just fine as he had a sweet tooth, his favourite being a homemade lemon drizzle cake.

A tear cascaded down my cheek. I wiped it away quickly, checking no one had noticed. I wondered had my parents survived that night, or were they slaughtered by the brothers. The latter must be true, because otherwise, why hadn't they found me, why hadn't I been rescued yet?

It had been nearly three years now, almost three years of sharing my body with desperate old men, names unknown, all in payment to the Payne brothers. The thought of which made me shudder.

I glanced over at the perfectly red roses glistening under the sunlit sky. Such perfection. They allow nothing but excellence here.

Beth had said maybe our parents were alive. Maybe they couldn't get in like we couldn't get out. She said even after all this time, we couldn't give up hope.

I smiled as I watched Jess and Beth dancing among the daisies, their nightdresses swirling and twirling much to the brother's delight. The three Payne brothers were sat at the other end of this part of the grounds watching us from their chairs, beers in hand, smoking.

Natasha sat beside the rose bushes, which suited her prickly exterior, but if you got close enough, she was kind at heart. She was picking at the blades of grass, trying to make music out of them. I'm not sure how, but I'm sure it was something my mother had shown me when I was younger. I walked up and plonked myself down beside her.

"Have you managed it yet?" I asked.

"Not yet, but I will," she said, determined. I smiled.

"So, why do you think they let us out today?"

She looked at me. "Because they want us to be happy. It means they've got something planned, and need us to be pliable for it."

I shuddered, dreading to think what it was.

"I heard Stefan tell Edison there will be another girl coming tonight."

"So soon?"

She nodded.

"But they already got rid of Laney's bed."

"That's what concerns me," Natasha said.

Shit. If Natasha was concerned. We should all be concerned!

The Payne brothers stood up. Edison

whistled and the four of us lined up ready to go in quietly.

***

The rest of the day they had left us alone. Granted the door was locked, and no food was served. But we were alone at least. The problem was, that Edison had told us the reason why we were to be left alone. He expected our bodies to be scrubbed clean. Our hair must shine, and be curled to perfection. We were to wear the skimpy underwear they had laid out for us on our beds, which for a change included pants.

"Is it another party?" Beth groaned, asking Natasha. She was always the one the girls would go to for information, and the one the brothers would speak to to arrange anything with us.

She nodded. "It's in preparation for the next hunt."

I shuddered.

"What are they hunting?" I asked, fearful of the answer. The main reason I asked is because I knew of the new girl coming tonight and I could have sworn I heard the cries of more than just Laney last night.

"Do you think that's where Laney was taken?" Beth asked. Her inquisitive nature always gets the better of her.

Jess's eyes widened. She came over and sat beside Beth, as I continued to curl her hair. "I hope not," I said. "If anything, I hope they gave her a quick death." She nodded.

Natasha huffed while painting her nails. "You know they wouldn't have Evie. Those sickos will do anything for a rise. And if it's a hunt they're preparing for, then I can guarantee Laney will be the prey they're hunting."

I narrowed my eyes at her as Beth gasped. "Well, she won't be much fun for them. She wanted to die. I can't see her running off screaming."

"That's the problem then isn't it!" Natasha said. "That's when they'll get angry and demand a second victim, and who do you think will be next?"

"What?" Beth cried.

"Well, we're going to right there in the middle of it serving drinks. They'll grab one of us."

My eyes widened. I knew she was right… we were fucked.

The room fell silent and Beth began to cry. "Hey none of that," Jess said, wiping her tears, "you'll ruin your make-up!" she nodded, sniffling. "Just you ignore her. We'll stick together you and me, I won't let them take you." I watched the two of them and knew the only way any of us got out of this was if I went in their place. Fuck.

Natasha finished blowing her nails, stood up and adjusted her bra. "Damn, these things don't half-pinch your skin!" I laughed. She was right. The brothers didn't know a thing about cup size!

"Come on, let's get this over and done with," I said. "Stick together!" Beth nodded, Jess too and Natasha looked at me with a knowing glance, then pushed to the front and banged on the door.

***

The dregs of humanity littered that room. A darkened space filled with ornate furniture, a pool table, a fully-stocked bar and men leering at us like we were pieces of meat and nothing more.

The dire stench of cigarettes and alcohol meshed with the sweat-filled randiness of old men wanting to get their rocks off, again and again, made my stomach heave. I saw Jess pulled aside by two men, her eyes pleading with them to let her go, but I knew by their sway, and the number of drinks we'd served them tonight, that there was no getting away from what they were about to do to her.

This party was no ordinary shindig. This was a civilised gathering, turned into a piss-up, turned into an orgy slash rape fest.

I did hope though for Jess's sake and for all

our sakes that the men who were now staring down at us like animals, would take their share then leave us alone and allow us to escape back to our quarters. But I doubted that would be the case.

"Hold up fellas!" Edison yelled, pulling one of the men off of Jess. "We've got more pressing matters to attend to first.

The man growled at him and hit his hand away. Edison laughed.

"Don't you remember the pretty little princess in the woods that needs hunting?" he yelled as the music dimmed and the room silenced at the sound of his voice.

The girls and I stood still, jaw dropped. Jess was busy trying to piece together her bra strap that they had broken. I took this time while they were busy yelling for glee and jumping about getting ready for their hunt to shimmy over to Jess and help her fix her strap. Beth and Natasha headed for us too. All of us headed to the back of the room, sticking together just as we said we would.

At the other end, each of the vile men had geared up with axes, swords, daggers, heck, even nets, which considering how drunk they were, they'd probably get themselves caught in. Edison, Stefan and Xander though… they were going to be the problem. They were stone-cold sober. The concentration in their eyes brought fear to mine. They enjoyed this, not just for the fun of it, but they took it seriously. The Midnight Hunt was a sport to them, a sick sport they had invested in.

I wonder if that's where all of the girls go. The ones that disappear in the middle of the night. The ones that cry too much, or scream or answer back. Perhaps they end up strung up somewhere in those woods at the back of the house. Is that where Laney is now? Will she be strung up too, left to rot so the birds can pick her apart? I shuddered. How could she want that? How can that be better than what we have right now? At least we still have that inkling of hope of escaping albeit a tiny one.

The glass double doors opened and the men filtered out, forgetting we were still there. I breathed a sigh of relief. But it was too little too late, as just as we turned ready to leave, I heard an almighty roar, a sickening thud and Laney's head was thrown through the glass door laying down in front of us.

A bloodied Edison stepped through the shattered glass door. "She didn't even fucking run," he said, his face framed with ferocity.

My eyes widened and I pushed Beth behind me. Natasha did the same with Jess. He looked over at us and grinned. An evil thought had crossed his mind as his footsteps pounded the floor one by one, drawing ever closer, until eventually, he stood towering over me.

"YOU!" he said, looking to Natasha.

"What!" she said, her eyes wide.

"NO!" I yelled, punching and kicking him.

"You can't have her!" I jumped on his back and scratched his face. He laughed, grabbing me by the hair and yanking me off.

"Oh Babydoll, I may not be able to touch you, but my father never said they couldn't!" He laughed, pushing Natasha over, picking me up, and flinging me over his shoulder, taking me out into the night.

ANNALEE ADAMS - WOLF

4

My heart hammered in my chest, the rhythm pulsing to a dance of death that enthralled my body, coursing adrenaline through it as my fight or flight kicked in. It was now or never. If tonight was going to be my last night on this Earth, I'd take every last one of them down with me.

Eddison's grip was like a vice as he threw me to the ground, my body slamming against the unforgiving earth. I lay there gasping for air, feeling like discarded trash, insignificant and worthless in his eyes. The ground beneath me was parched and unyielding, thanks to the Summertime drought we'd had as of late.

The earthy scent of the forest filled my nostrils, mixed with the metallic tang of fear and the stale smell of my sweat. The scent of danger lingered in the air, a warning that the forest was no longer a safe place.

My determination to survive this hunting trip burned fiercely within me, even as my bruised bottom throbbed in pain from Eddison's rough handling. I winced, rubbing it.

I planned to survive this fuck up of a hunting trip, especially if the brothers weren't allowed to touch me. All I had to do was outsmart the heavily intoxicated men who crowded around me with their sharpened weapons glinting in the dim light. All I needed was to find a weapon of my own and then bide my time, watching their every move. My plan seemed foolproof in theory.

I braced myself against the biting wind, feeling exposed and vulnerable in nothing but my pale pink underwear. It was a constant reminder of how little control we had over our bodies. The dress code they imposed on us was suffocating and degrading, yet I couldn't bear the thought of facing the consequences if I didn't comply. My mind and body were at war, torn between standing up for my beliefs and conforming to their twisted standards.

Standing up, I stood in the darkness surrounded by a pack of wolves, wolves made of men with leering glances, yet all all I had to defend myself with was my fists. I should be scared. But instead, I was too busy figuring out which one was the largest. He'd be the slowest runner, but I'd better stay away from his club as it was sure to pack a punch. The one that had been tossing back whiskeys all night though, he was my target. The slick businessman with the Southern accent and greasy hair… his axe would sure come in handy.

I narrowed my gaze, glaring from one Payne brother to the other. They circled like predators,

Edison's sick grin, Stefan's unsettling glare, and Xander's cruel laughter raising the hairs on my arms. Their perverse glee as they scented my fear was palpable, as if it were a tangible thing, coating the chilling night air. I pushed back as they came closer, determined to fight to the death.

Xander's eyes narrowed, a predatory edge to his soulless glare. "Feisty, aren't we?" He said, smirking, grabbing my chin and forcing me to meet his lifeless gaze. "That'll change soon enough." His leering smirk, more animal than human, sent a shiver down my spine.

"Back it up men," Edison yelled. They snarled but did as they were told. "Now, welcome to our Midnight Hunt," he drawled, his voice slithering through the night like icy tendrils creeping down your spine. "Babydoll…" he looked at me and I glared at him, fear taking a backseat to my anger at that moment. "Run…"

Shit! I would have thought he would have counted down from three or something! It took me a moment to process the word. But as soon as I did, I was out of there.

The hunt was a frantic dance of survival, with each footstep screaming out against the deafening silence of the forest, and the menacing shadows reaching out like twisted hands. Fallen trees were hurdles that scraped against my fear, pushing me forward, and leaving a trail of rustling leaves and snapping branches behind me.

Zigzagging between the trees, I stopped to catch my breath. Glancing back, I could see Stefan and Xander, their flashlights like demonic eyes in the distance, fanning out to noose me in. Granted they couldn't hurt me, but they would be happy to make me an easy target for their hunting party.

As I pushed further into the dark, the air grew thicker and more oppressive, constricting my throat and weighing down on my chest. It was nearly impossible to breathe. Instead, I focused on the musty smell of decomposition and pine, reminding myself that this was my reality now. After a few deep breaths, I pressed on, determined to conquer whatever lay ahead.

The trees concealed me for now, but it was only a matter of time before my hunters closed in. Shit! I needed a plan! The greasy-haired Southern businessman was too far away, so there was no chance of getting his weapon, and the only weapons around here were fallen branches that wouldn't last five minutes against swords and axes, especially considering how dry it's been out here lately! My mind whirled, desperate with ideas. Biting my lower lip I was angry. Furious in fact. Damn it. I won't go down without a fight! I had to use the one thing I never wanted to use.

I sighed, looked left to right, checked no one was around and ran as fast as I could. I guess they expected me to continue running through the forest, screaming and crying like a little princess begging for mercy. No. I'd had almost three damned years of this shit. This abuse. This hatred as it boiled up inside. There was no way they were taking me down that easily. The greasy-haired guy was too far back now, and the men with the nets had taken the lead. The last thing I wanted was to be caught in their trap. So I headed for the mansion. Because I knew, if I made it there. There was a chance he would be there. He would see. He was the only chance I had right now. Daddy.

The light ahead blared out a beacon of hope. I never thought I'd prey to make it back to that place in one piece, but I did.

The brothers' mad laughter echoed through the dense forest, sending chills down my spine. My heart thumped wildly in my chest as I sprinted through the trees, their cackles getting closer with each passing moment. My legs burned with exhaustion, but I refused to slow down. I could see a gnarled oak up ahead and dove behind it, hoping to catch my breath and come up with a plan.

The brothers closed in, their cruel laughter echoing around me. Looking around frantically, I searched for anything to use. I'm small, but I'm quick. I have to use that to my advantage.

Footsteps crashed through the underbrush behind me, hot on my heels. My breath came in ragged gasps, as I bolted forward, my bare feet bled from the sharp rocks and tangled roots that littered the forest floor. But I couldn't stop now. Searching for any sign of a way out, I begged any higher power to save my ass this one time and show me a way to escape this twisted game.

Ahead, I finally saw him, Daddy, as he walked towards the forest, his masked face unnerving but strangely comforting in this sea of terror. He spotted me and our eyes locked. For a brief moment, I almost wept with relief. He held a finger to his lips, signalling for me to be quiet.

With a nod from Daddy, I cautiously emerged from our hiding spot. The lingering smell of the Payne brothers' cigarettes invaded my senses. Were they still close? My body trembled, heart pounding, as the metallic taste of fear coated my tongue. Each breath came thick and heavy, the adrenaline a bitter aftertaste as it surged through my veins, pushing me forward, and propelling me away from the woods and into his arms.

Daddy crept along the shadows, leading the way. The full moon casts a foreboding glow, illuminating the twisted path before us, a secret path he once showed me as a means to escape the gardens and enter the mansion through the cellar.

"Why are you running from them?" I asked him, confused. He was usually in control, and I'd expected him to reprimand them for what they were doing to me and the other girls. Did he not care? He stopped, turned around and slapped me.

"You do not have time to ask questions Babydoll. The hunters will kill you if they find you out here, and I cannot control all of them."

I nodded, a tear glistening in my eye as I rubbed my red cheek.

He huffed, grabbed my hand and pulled me along after him.

As we left the canopy of the forest, the first light of dawn crept across the landscape, promising freedom and salvation, at least for now. Relief began to flood through me, only to be replaced by icy fear. The Payne brothers won't be far behind. We're running out of time.

"We're almost there," Daddy bit out, his voice a ghostly wind in my ear. Almost there… back to being trapped, raped and abused. Part of me understood Laney's choice. Her delight in that final smile as she was chosen as the sacrificial lamb for the slaughter. I took a deep breath, walked up the path, and Daddy opened the door and pulled me into the abysmal pit of darkness once more.

5

Running through the cellar tunnels I watched Daddy run in front leading the way. It was a labyrinth of hellish proportions down here. Once built and used for slavers back in the 1800's. My mind wandered to the history of the place, and the journies those people must have been on. Had they suffered like I had? Perhaps they had endured worse than I at the hands of the Payne family. Was Beth right though, did anyone get out of here like she believed they did? Did they use these tunnels to escape? Part of me wanted to throw down bread crumbs like Hansel and Gretel, but no doubt the rats would gobble them up before sunset and we'd have no such luck at escape. It looked like for now, my only way forward was to follow Daddy's footsteps and hope he kept me safe… just as he always had.

I still do wonder why he keeps me safe. I know Natasha said she overhead the brothers talking about their missing sister. Maybe I remind him of her. But to be honest, anyone who lets their daughter endure this type of abuse should be hung, drawn and quartered. If only we still had that torture device available. I bet the Payne brothers have one somewhere down here…

I panted as Daddy picked up speed and I continued to hobble along, my feet still hurting from the cuts and scrapes. I still remember back to when he first stopped Edison that day. I remember wondering why. But what I always found peculiar, and eventually just learned to accept it, was the invitation.

So, nearly three years ago, when I had just been taken after Daddy put Edison back in his place and the girls and I had formed a sisterly bond, I was sat in our room thinking about the haunted house of horror we lived in. The mansion was the epitome of terror, with its walls crumbling with the rot of the Payne brothers' sins.

I'd been trapped there for days by then, each one more gruesome than the last. The smell of blood and sweat permeated the air, an inescapable reminder of my captivity.

I shifted in the darkness, my body ached from Edison's abuse, but it was nothing compared to the fear that gnawed at me. The previous events replayed in my mind like a horror movie on repeat - the kidnapping, the beatings, the snuff film he attempted to reenact with me as the star. It was a nightmare come to life.

That's when I heard them. His footsteps, heavy and deliberate, thudded down the hallway. The sound sent a shiver down my spine. It wasn't Edison; his steps were lighter, more predatory.

These belonged to someone else entirely. The girls fled and I froze, still sitting on my bed, in the middle of plaiting my red hair.

The door swung open, flooding the room with harsh light. A silhouette stood in the doorway, a man so imposing that even though he wore a mask, his presence was overwhelming. His eyes were hidden behind the dark fabric, but I could feel them boring into me, assessing me as if I were a specimen under a microscope.

The last time I had laid eyes on this man he had thrown Edison to the floor for trying to kill me. That was the first of many times his sons tried to murder me. But on this occasion, the first occasion, this time he was here with an invitation.

"Babydoll," he said, walking over and towering over me.

The air grew heavy with the weight of his presence. I sat there, unmoving. "No," he says, and slaps my hand away from the plait in my hair, yanking my plait undone. "This will not do. You will leave your hair as it was!"

My eyes widened and I bit my trembling lip. He looked at me. "Oh. I see I have upset you."

Extending his hand towards me, his fingers outstretched like talons, "Come," he said, and even with the voice changer he used, his voice seemed somewhat softer, yet still underlined with authority. "You are to join me for dinner."

I flinched at his touch. He sighed, which seemed to echo through the silent room, as the girls remained hidden away. He withdrew his hand. His expression was saddened. "It's going to take time for you to trust me," he said. "But you will. You are mine now. Now stand up Babydoll. It is rude to turn down an invite."

My eyes widened more and I began to stand shakily. He pulled me up. "There, see. That wasn't too hard, was it? Now follow me." He turned on his heel and walked out of the room. I turned to face the hidden girls. Natasha shrugged and Jess ushered me to follow him quickly, so I did.

As we walked through the darkened halls of the mansion. He spoke to me in low tones, his voice almost a whisper as he shared his knowledge of the Payne brothers' routines and weaknesses. It was an intimate moment, one that felt both surreal and strangely comforting. He explained he was telling me this to prevent me from being a victim. I never understood why.

When we entered the dining areas, I remember how astounded I was at the minimalist approach he had taken in the room. There was nothing but a vast space with a long, ornate dining table in the centre that seated ten people.

He ushered me forward and pulled out a chair at one end of the table, I sat and he pushed the seat in, allowing me to sit closer still. But as he did, his cold hand, the hand that bore the remnants of an aged broken heart tattoo brushed through my hair and over my shoulder. I gasped and he walked off, seating himself at the opposite end, shrouded by darkness.

The only light in this room was the candlelight that adorned my place setting. A four-piece golden candelabra stood right in front of me, illuminating the many knives and forks, the serviette shaped like a fan, and the five spoons that I had no idea what to do with.

I gazed through the flicker of flames trying to ascertain his figure, but alas all I could see was a faint shadow moving beyond the light.

The first course was served. Butternut squash with ravioli had a buttery taste and oh my lord it was exquisite. My mother was an exceptional cook, but she had never cooked her ravioli like this. There were herbs added in, a sprig of rosemary from what I could make out. The only reason I remembered was due to my father's love of gardening. I sighed, thinking back to them.

The man called Daddy never spoke, instead, all I could hear was the soft clatter of the occasional implement used to eat with, or perhaps a delicate sip of wine with the meal.

By the following course, I had decided he wasn't going to murder me. If he was, he wouldn't be wasting glazed lamb chops with roasted vegetables and a hearty white bean puree, would he? I thought it was a fair conclusion, and I was right. Because that evening Daddy and I came to an understanding. I remained silent, and he remained my protector. There was no rhyme or reason behind it.

Finishing my main meal I stretched out in my seat, taking a small sip of wine. Now for a, well, I was thirteen at the time, with no experience of alcohol, well… it went straight to my head. I hardly recall the desert after that considering my vision turned hazy and all hell broke loose in my wild and wicked imagination. It was either that or one of the brothers had drugged me to have their wicked way without even me knowing.

Sitting in the chair I span, the flames from the candelabra swirling and twirling before my eyes, dancing a poetic dance to the invisible notes that caressed the airwaves. Shadows stretched like long, grasping fingers across the walls of the cavernous room, playing tricks on my vision. Each creak and whisper of this ancient mansion sent a shiver down my spine, as if the house itself was alive, breathing with a sinister pulse. I wrapped my arms around myself, feeling the chill of the night seep through the thin fabric of my night dress. The moon's glow filtered through the gap in the midnight curtains, casting an eerie pallor on my skin. A glow which soon became consumed by the hand that reached me, the hand with the broken heart tattoo, the one whose eyes angered as he gripped my chin, turning my head from side to side and yelling for his sons. That was the night he told them I was off limits. That was the night he saved me again.

I sighed. It seems he does a lot of saving me

around here. Yet in almost three years, I have still never seen his face. At least tonight I heard his voice, even if it was mumbled and from a distance.

"It's through here," he said, through the voice changer. I nodded, remaining silent.

Following him, we came to a door that required an old key. Daddy pulled out a set of keys and unlocked it, and as he did I could hear the mechanism grinding as the levers lined up, unlocking the door. I watched, taking it all in, making a mental note that if we were to get out of this place we would need to get hold of that key. I wondered who else would have a copy.

"Come on," he said, stepping into what appeared to be the kitchen. I stepped through, and he locked the door behind us.

I nodded. "May I ask a question?" He nodded. "The brothers will be out for blood. How can I keep myself and my girls safe from them?"

He huffed. "You can't." I sighed, shaking my head. "But," he said, motioning for me to sit at the kitchen table. "I will smooth this over with the people that came to their gathering." He tapped his fingers on the table, taking a moment to consider his options. "I will also take my boys away for two weeks to reprimand them, and remind them what Payne Industries is about."

"What is it about?"

He smiled. "Pleasure." I shuddered. "Some might say they found the hunt pleasurable. But that is saved for the bad girls, for those not welcome in the family. You are not one of those girls Babydoll. You are mine." I shuddered again.

"Now, back to your room, my sons will be gone when you awaken. But make no mistake, you will still be watched."

I nodded and hurried back to the room.

ANNALEE ADAMS - WOLF

6

Two weeks of pure bliss commenced. It was perfect. Days were spent sunbathing, laughing together, taking picnics out in the gardens and not panicking at every footstep, cry or bang in the night.

Granted we were still reined in by the likes of the uncle, who leered at us from the corner of the room or crept among the shadows late at night. He had never touched any of us, but his whole persona was far from endearing. With his dark ginger hair and cast-iron stare he was the opposite of what I thought Daddy would look like under that mask.

Picnicking out in the garden, one of the servants bought our dinner for us. Daddy had ensured we were served only the finest foods during these two weeks, and treated like guests rather than victims. I watched as the solemn-faced pale servant laid down the tray, his thin bony hands shaking. He was a picture of mistreatment too. I often wondered if the servants got to go home. But, looking at this poor chap, he certainly didn't.

The guards though, they're paid employees. They never speak, just watch and wait, roaming the grounds with their attack dogs on leads. I'd hate to be caught by one of them on an escape attempt. They'd have no problem in ripping me to shreds.

"It's nice Evie, eat up," Jess said, motioning to the food on the picnic blanket in front of me. I smiled. I hadn't much of an appetite since I saw what happened to Laney. After witnessing murder it's hard to keep hope in your heart. Especially when tomorrow it could be any one of us.

I nodded, picked up my steak sandwich and took a bite. She was right. The food was scrumptious. I closed my eyes, took a deep breath and gobbled up my plateful of food. Beth laughed watching me.

When I opened my eyes I could see Natasha studying me, taking a small bite of her sandwich. "So are you going to tell us what happened then?" she asked. "As it's sure got you worked up."

I wiped my mouth on the back of my hand, bit my lower lip and looked down, picking at the fluff on the blanket. "All you need to know is that we all have to get out of this place, like, now." My eyes widened as I said the last part, the alarming feeling still building inside of me.

"You know there's no way out Evie," she said. "We've searched."

"That's where you're wrong," I said, smiling slightly. "When Daddy saved me from them, he showed me a way through the labyrinth below the mansion. It used to be used to hide slaves in the past. He said it splits off so the families that lived here could escape should they ever need to."

"Huh?" Beth said.

"What?"

Jess looked at me mouth agape. "Did he just tell you how to escape?"

"No, he wouldn't," Natasha said.

"I said to him that the brothers would be out for my blood now. That's when he told me that."

"So, what he wants you to use the tunnels?"

I shrugged. "He must do."

"Why the hell didn't you tell us this?" Natasha almost yelled.

Jess shushed her.

"Because," I said. "There's one catch."

"Of course there is!"

"To leave the mansion you have to go through an old door in the kitchen. It's always locked."

"Okay, so where's the key."

"Well, he even showed me the key, how ornate and beautiful it was. I think that was so I would know what it looked like."

"He was leaving all the breadcrumbs wasn't he!" Jess exclaimed. I nodded. "So where's the key?"

"Well, he has one. The brothers have one…"

"They're not here," Beth groaned.

"Exactly that's a good thing," I said. "He gave us two weeks."

"But how do we get a key if they're not here?"

"Because who else is here with a set of keys?" I said, grinning like a Cheshire Cat. I had figured it out while I'd sat there playing with the picnic blanket, piecing everything together.

"The Uncle!" Natasha stated, her lips creasing in the corners, her eyes narrowing into a knowing look. "We have to take it from the uncle." I nodded.

Jess and Beth remained quiet. Beth continued picking at the grass, while Jess stared up at the clouds thinking.

"Okay," Natasha said. "We do it tomorrow when he's watching us dress."

I shuddered. "Eurgh, he watches us dress?" How had I not known that?

"Yes, he has done for years. Haven't you seen the holes strategically placed in our bedroom wall?" My steak sandwich threatened to come back up again.

"But how is he looking through them? From what room?"

"I don't know. But I say, we get ready and when we see him peering through we shove something sharp through the hole into his eye."

Beth turned pale.

"What?" Natasha said. "He deserves it."

"He's the only one that's never touched us," Jess said.

"Give him time!"

"Don't get me wrong, the guy gives me the creeps, but I wasn't planning on killing him," I said. "The brothers most definitely, but not him. He never did anything to hurt me."

"Well, how else are we going to get that key?"

"One of us could distract him, while the other grabs the key?" Jess suggested.

"That could go hideously wrong," Natasha said.

"Better than stabbing someone in the eye!" Jess cried.

"Fine. We can try that this afternoon, but if it goes tits up, then we're stabbing him in the eye," Natasha huffed.

I rolled my eyes. "Fine," I agreed. Jess folded her arms.

Natasha stood up. "Come on then, no time like the present."

Beth was about to take a bit out of her sandwich when Natasha grabbed her hand and pulled her up.

"But!" she said, looking at her plate of food.

"No buts! Just think about all the food you can have when we get out of here!"

I smirked at Beth's disappointment at her lowly sandwich going to waste as we walked off back toward the mansion.

Trailing through the mansion, we found certain rooms remained locked. One of which was his room. Eddisons. I shuddered as snippets of my past flickered through my mind. The bed frame, the knife play, and the intensive studio lighting made your skin feel like it would melt off at any moment. The lights always intensified everything. They made you so hot, sweat running from your body in a wild panic. The metallic tang of fear choked me as it hit the back of my throat.

I was back there again, as I stood staring at that locked doorway. On the outside, it appeared a normal white wooden door, etched with a Fleur De Lyes pattern and intricate golden details. It looked elegant. Pleasant even. But inside I was thrown straight back into my worst nightmare… tied up, stripped bare and being filmed for their pleasure.

My life up until now was one of desperation, clumsily scratching at the darkness of my mind, pleading for a way out. Even if we did make it out of here alive, I knew, I would always be that girl tied to this bed, exposed and abused over and over again. At least until I killed every single one of them… then at least I'd feel somewhat better perhaps. I sighed, shrugged and caught up with the other girls.

"Where is he?" I questioned, puzzled after we'd searched the kitchen, dining area and the three living spaces we knew he liked to hang out in. Jess shrugged.

"Perhaps he's up there," Natasha said, pointing upstairs. I looked up and paled. We'd never been upstairs before, and it wasn't somewhere I fancied venturing. For if they caught us up there it would mean certain death. The upstairs was explicitly out of bounds and only for members of the Payne family.

Behind me the clock chimed six in the evening, making me jump. Natasha stifled a laugh. "So, are we going then?" she asked. I gulped. Even I wasn't that stupid. Escaping was one thing, but running upstairs where there was no way out scared the life out of me. Especially considering we don't know what the hell else lived up there.

"I'm good with waiting for him to come down here."

She narrowed her eyes. "You do know the brothers are back tomorrow."

"What the heck…" I replied. "I thought it was the day after!"

"No, it's tomorrow."

"Well, technically it depends if you take the two weeks as when Daddy said it or starting from the day after when they left," Jess said, pursing her lips, thinking.

I took a deep breath. We couldn't risk the chance of waiting. "Damn it. We've got to go up." God, I hated my life.

Natasha smiled, grabbed the bannister so hard her palm whitened, and then led the way.

With a breath that was filled with more determination than air, I stepped away from the sanctuary of what I knew on the ground floor and took my first step upstairs. My feet found silent purchase on the cold floor of each wooden step.

As we reached the top, every fibre of my being strained against the urge to run, to give in to pure panic. Instead, I moved with purpose, a silent spectre drifting through the corridors where dread and secrecy mingled like toxic perfume.

I pressed my back against the cool, uneven

surface of the corridor wall, every sense sharpened to a needle's point. My gaze flitted from shadow to shadow, as we searched along the corridor, peering inside each open door to find empty rooms full of unused furniture gathering dust, or locked doors tempting the imagination deep within.

The mansion loomed around us, its gilded edges and velvet drapes a mockery of comfort. I lead the girls through the echoing halls, each step deliberate, and measured. Our eyes darted to every shadow, every whisper of movement that might betray another soul's presence—or something far worse.

"Keep close," I breathed, my voice barely more than a rustle against the oppressive silence. I could feel the thrumming of my heartbeat, a rhythm that tapped in time with our soft footsteps.

It was only moments later we could hear the straining laughter of the old man we knew to be the uncle, Daddy's brother. He was the perverted owner of this mansion, who appeared slow and the very presence of him creeped me out. Natasha nodded, pointing in the direction of what I presumed was his bedroom. The four of us crept forward and paused beside his door.

What was the plan? Did we even have one?

The door creaked open and instantly the uncle stopped laughing. We stepped across the threshold, the weight of dread settling on my shoulders like a leaden cloak.

The air inside was stale, charged with the stagnant energy of secrets long buried. I could almost taste the fear that lingered here, an acrid tang on the tip of my tongue.

Flickering light from the television cast shadows that danced upon the walls, contorting into grotesque shapes that followed our footsteps.

With each timid step forward, the room revealed itself—an altar of atrocities hidden within these prison walls, with the uncle sitting in the centre. He may have been the quietest of the bunch. But the uncle was by far the sickest.

I turned, slowly, taking in the full horror of the room. Bondage gear hung solemnly from hooks on the walls, leather straps and metal chains drape like morbid decorations. It's a museum of pain, each piece a testament to the suffering we've endured at the hands of those who see us as nothing more than playthings. Seeing them displayed so openly, so unashamedly, sends a tremor of disgust through me. Yet who did he bring here? None of us were allowed upstairs. What disturbed me the most was the bloodied pair of gloves and heavy-duty bin bags heaving to the brim in the far corner. What the hell did he have in those?

"God," Beth said, grabbing me, her voice barely above a whisper.

We stood rooted to the spot, a collective statue of terror. Yet, beneath the surface ran a current of anger, hot and unforgiving. This room, this shrine to our captivity, ignited something fierce within me—a flame that will not be smothered until we have clawed our way out of this nightmare.

"Pretty girls…" the uncle said, standing up, smiling and rubbing his hands together. "You're not meant to be up here."

"Yes," Natasha says. Her voice wavering slightly. "But we wanted to see you, Robert."

"Why did you want to see Robert?"

"Well because…" then she turned and looked at us, her eyes wide. She had nothing.

My eyes widened. "Because," I said, continuing. "We hadn't seen you all day Robert," I took a few steps towards him, noting the keys that hung from his belt. "We wanted to make sure you were okay."

"Robert is okay!" He smiled. "Robert likes to watch this programme at this time. Do you like this programme?"

Jess walked forward, so she could see the television. "No," she said. "What is it?"

Natasha and I walked over to Robert and pretended to cuddle him from either side, sitting down on the edge of the bed together. "Can we watch it with you Robert?" I asked.

He nodded. "Yes, Robert would like that. But do not tell my brothers. They do not like it when Robert plays with girls in here. As Robert makes a mess." I gulped, looking at the bin bags and deciding not to question it any further. Part of me wondered if that's where the new girl ended up.

Beth remained and stood back in the shadows. I didn't blame her. She was too scared.

Jess continued to talk to Robert about the television show while Natasha cuddled into Robert's neck and I tried to slowly remove the keys from his belt without him noticing. It felt like it was taking forever, and I almost bloody had it too, then an advert came on and Robert got up.

"I need a wee break. You girls stay there," he said, standing up. But as he did, the keys slipped off of his now undone belt, out of my hand and onto the floor. He looked down, looked at his belt, at the keys, then at me and roared.

With a face of thunder, eyes wide, body stiff he drew back his fist and punched out, barely missing my face. Jess pulled me to the side just in time. Natasha jumped on the back of him. She'd managed to grab one of the bondage ropes, but even with how tall she was, he was twice as big, at least twice as strong and had more muscle than any boxer I'd ever seen. What the hell had they been feeding this guy? Natasha wouldn't stand a chance!

I ran over to his selection of toys and took his dagger, thrusting it into his side. He groaned as I stabbed him, and it wasn't easy to do that. Just the thrusting in of the blade was like puncturing a rubber tyre filled with plasticine. He grabbed the wound as I pulled out the knife. I pushed it forward again, this time catching his hand in the process, pinning it in place. I left the knife there, instead grabbing the baseball bat and whacking him with it until he eventually went down.

Jess was already kicking him, whereas Natasha was still strangling him. Beth just looked on in horror. By now though a pool of blood had flowed out from his heavy-duty bin bags and merged with his. So, it looked like my suspicions of his late-night activities, most likely with the new girl had ended up with her chopped up and thrown away like rubbish. I never imagined he'd be this sick in the head though. I always knew he was a pervert, but that's as far as it went. He always seemed scared of the brothers to dare try anything. I took a deep breath and sighed, looking down at his dead body, and our now bloodied nightdresses.

Natasha grabbed the keys and we made our way back to the kitchen as quickly as we could before anyone could see us, or alert security of the uncle's quick departure. I trembled.

There were that many keys and I couldn't remember which bloody one it was. There was one golden one with a swirl on the handle, that didn't work. The next was a silver ornate key. That didn't work either. Then a beautiful elegant key, I could almost hear the levers groaning inside, but it was all to taunt us as it gave up halfway through. I almost kicked the damn door down by the tenth key.

"Fucks sake!" Natasha said, grabbing the keys off of me. Then the first key she tried the bloody door opened. Typical!

It was no cause for celebration though. It was no time for escape. Right there on the other side of the door, staring right at us, as we stood in our bloodied nightdresses were the Payne brothers and their Daddy, returning early from their trip away.

"Evening Babydoll, now just where do you

think you're going dressed like that?" Edison said.

7

Without a thought, I bolted past them into the labyrinth of tunnels beyond. The girls followed. It did cross my mind that any one of them could have grabbed us, but instead, they laughed as we ran, enjoying the hunt.

Beth squealed as she ran, darting past me but taking a wrong turn to the left instead of the right. At least I think that was the wrong way. I would have shrugged except for all the intense panting as the adrenaline coursed through my veins.

Fear gripped at my throat, causing it to constrict. Bile forcibly reached up into my mouth making me gag. I was a panic-stricken mess, as I knew if they caught us, there would be no coming back from this.

Behind me, I could hear the hard pounding of footsteps as one of the Payne brothers chased me. Where were the other girls? None of them had made it past me since Beth did. Had they all taken the left corridor? Was I the one in the wrong? I gulped, pushing forward, struggling to see with the minimal lighting the odd lantern here and there gave out. They gave the atmosphere an even spookier feel, which was not the vibe I needed right now.

Trailing down the tunnel I had to slow down. The footsteps were in the distance by now, and considering I had taken many turns here and there I was as lost as they probably were. So instead, I decided to try and get my bearings, study the dirt walls and see if there were any signs of life, any inkling of water feeding the roots of plants, or well anything. If there was, then we'd be under the forest, which was the right direction. But there was nothing but dried-up old dirt and wooden beams holding the tunnel together. This place reminded me of an old mining tunnel, minus the rails, cart or expensive gemstones.

I had been walking another ten, possibly fifteen minutes when I heard a scream. It stunned me to silence. I stopped, tensed and prayed they were okay. That we'd all come out of this unscathed. Although in my heart of hearts, I knew that part was a lie.

Up ahead the tunnel appeared to get brighter, not by natural light, although I wish it was! No, there seemed to be more lanterns in this section.

As I walked up to the brighter area, I found a large hollowed-out cavern on the side of the dirt path. My brow furrowed. Why was there a cavern down here? Did the slaves used to live down here under the mansion?

Ahead of me, the dirt walls rose high, a good

ten, maybe twelve feet. Which meant only one thing… I had ventured deeper underground without even knowing it.

Within the vast space, there were wooden tables and an old framed bed with crumpled sheets.

Cobwebs festered over the wooden headboard like macabre lace, but the mattress itself looked recently used.

In each of the four corners, sections were splintered off, and besides those, there were what appeared to be dried blood stains. Was this where the brothers held some of their girls? I thought we were the only ones, but maybe they took more just for whatever this place was.

Walking around the bed I came to one of the tables. With each stride, the air grew less oppressive, the shadows less menacing.

Beside the bed stood a shelving unit laden with jars, untouched for quite some time. I picked one of the largest jars up and yelped placing it back down. Inside, staring back at me was the fetus of an unborn child with wide eyes open and alert. I did not dare identify what was in the other jars. The sight of them twisted my stomach in knots, yet it's the photographs that drew me closer—a macabre gallery of the brothers' exploits, each snapshot a testament to their cruelty.

I looked from one grisly image to another: faces twisted in agony, bodies contorted in unnatural positions, eyes that will never see again reflecting the flash of the camera.

The room began to spin, and bile rose in my throat. These are not just crimes; they are perversions of human suffering, captured and displayed for some disgusting sick sense of accomplishment.

I struggled to breathe, the weight of the horrors threatening to crush me. But amidst the darkness, a fire ignited within, hot and fierce. I will not let the terror paralyse me—not when escape is so close, not when justice hangs in the balance.

There was a rustle, a displacement of air, and I froze. Is it them? Have I been discovered? A rat skittered across the floor, as eager to escape as I was, and I breathed again. I see a mirror of my desperation in its small, scurrying form.

My breath catches as my gaze fell upon the cameras. They perched like silent vultures throughout the room, their lenses cold and unblinking. Each one is positioned with purpose, methodically arranged to capture every angle of torment that has unfolded in this space. My skin prickles with the violation of it, the realisation that the victim's darkest moments have been recorded, immortalised by these mechanical eyes. It's as if they watch me now, hungry for more scenes of despair to add to their collection.

On one of the tables, my fingers brushed against the spine of a journal, its cover leathery and worn like the skin of an old apple. I pulled it from its resting place between two dust-laden books. Each page I turned crackled with the weight of its history as if protesting the unveiling of its secrets.

Picking it up, I walked over to one of the lanterns so I could read it.

'"July 2012,"' it said, as I read aloud in a strained whisper.

'Rebecca Evans. Blond. Slim build. Aged 15. Axe. Lasted 5:42 minutes.'

'Jane Simmons. Brunette. Average build. Aged 14. Knife play, then suffocation. Lasted 8:13 minutes.'

'Princess. No known surname. Redhead. Voluptuous. Aged 18. Dogs. Lasted 2:10 minutes.'

'Josie Jenkins. Brunette. Athletic build. Aged 16. Strangulation during sex. Lasted 7:56 minutes.'

'Tilly Byrone. Blond. Voluptuous. Aged 15. Xanders art. Time unknown.'

And the list went on. There were pages, all in different handwriting, all different months and years. These snuff films had been going on for as far back as the eighties. It looked like it started with Daddy's father. It could have even started before, maybe there were other journals, or perhaps they didn't record them back then. But the one thing I knew for sure. This journal was the key to taking down the whole damn family. I just needed to get it out of here first!

Setting the journal aside, I forced myself to look away, only to have my breath hitch at the sight before me—a collection of weapons meticulously arranged on a table like some grotesque display. Knives with blades that reflected the scant light, revealing their cruel edges. Chains lay coiled, serpentine and cold, waiting for flesh to bind.

I stepped closer, despite every instinct screaming for me to flee. Each instrument told a tale of torment, the polished surfaces hiding the truth of their use. A shiver cascaded down my spine as I imagined the pain they had inflicted, the powerlessness they had imposed.

The musty air hung heavy in the hidden room, clinging to my skin like a warning. The urge to reach out and run my fingers over the blades pulled me back to reality. These weapons had taken countless lives in the past. I couldn't let them take anymore.

Collecting as many as I could I armed myself, strapping on a belt with two daggers; one on either side of my bloodied nightdress. In my hands, I held two more daggers and placed the journal down my dress. I was damned well going to fight my way out of this place if it was the last thing I did!

Leaving the cavern I continued down

through the tunnels, unsure of which way I was going, which direction I had come from and how far underground I was. Realistically I was what you would call, screwed.

Trudging along, the tunnels all appeared the same. It was a dirt pathway through Hell. Nothing and nobody around. Thank God! But no salvation, no natural light and no bloody way out! Part of me wanted the Payne brothers to turn up, just so I could try out my new toys and try to kick their asses with the very knives they had used to slice the throats of so many young girls over the years.

I shuddered. They must get a kick out of it. The killing I mean. Why else would they do it? It's not like they need the money. This place was pretty much paid for and they're the richest family in the city. So why carry on profiting through people's misery? I never understood it.

They enjoyed the sex. I know Edison did. Xander liked the freaky shit and to be quite honest he had rarely touched me, but when he did he scared the crap out of me. He wasn't scary in a good way like what you would find in a dark romance novel. Oh no… Xander was scary like in a psychopathic serial killer novel. He seemed to fantasise about death and blood, he was obsessed with it. I swear he would rather the person he was banging had no pulse!

Turning yet another corner I heard footsteps and stopped dead still. Whispers caught my attention as shadows swayed under the lantern before me. Time slowed and I started to back up. The whispers stopped. Had they heard me? Each step felt like an eternity.

My heart careened against my ribcage, a bird trapped in a cage of betrayal. The air ripped from my lungs as the realisation crashed into me—I was outnumbered.

I bit my lower lip as the three brothers caught up to me. Stefan, Edison, and Xander loomed before me. Panic clawed at my throat, raw and desperate. The glimmer of hope that once flickered within me was snuffed out, leaving only the cold embrace of reality. No amount of knives would be enough against three of them!

Edison instantly thrusts his hand forward, dodging my feeble attempt at slashing him with one of the knives. Fingers like iron bands wrapped around my throat, squeezing the breath from me. I dropped the knives, clawing at his hand, trying to release it. My world narrowed to the pressure against my windpipe, the desperation clawing at my chest. Panic was a living thing within me, rearing up with wild eyes and flailing limbs. He lifted me by my neck, against the dirt wall and I kicked out, nails scratching into his skin.

Eyes widening. Face turning red, then purple. "Can't... breathe..." I wheezed, my voice no louder than a whisper lost in a storm.

My hands clawed at his vice-like grip, seeking purchase on something, anything. But it's like trying to bend steel with bare fingers. Black spots dance before my eyes, each one an echo of my pounding heart. This can't be how it ends. Not with so much left undone, not with freedom's taste still lingering on my lips.

I refuse to go quietly into that suffocating darkness. With every remaining shred of strength, I twisted and bucked beneath his hold, defiance burning through the haze of fear.

Then, as suddenly as it began, the assault ended, and I fell to the ground. My neck burned, leaving a trail of fire along my skin. Edison stepped back, his towering figure casting a shadow that felt as cold as the grave.

Air precious sweet air rushed into my lungs in ragged gasps. I crumpled to the ground, the impact sending tremors through my bruised body. I'm alive, but survival has never been so bittersweet.

Xander pulled me up off the floor and threw me over his shoulder. "You've been a naughty girl

Baby doll, we're going to have fun with you!"

8

Slipping into the surreal world of unconsciousness my mind wandered to a significant memory of my past here at the mansion. It must be around that time of year again, I thought, as Xander carried my limp body back through the tunnels. What had he done to me when he slung me over his shoulder? Surely the strangulation itself had not caused my mind to slipstream into the land of dreams. Fighting I tried to stay awake. Fearing that when I awoke I'd be chopped up in little pieces or starring in one of their warped snuff films.

The brothers were talking as they walked,

but speech came as a blurred language that mumbled into an incoherent splurge of syllables. Although I did see Edison grinning as he gripped my face and said something to his brothers. Had they drugged me? Injected me? I'd been so out of it after being on the verge of life and death that there's no way I could have known.

The only thing keeping me awake, and alive, was my thoughts. Deliberate messages between the past and the present.

As we stepped into the kitchen, the chill of the mansion's midnight air crept through calming me. But it's the memory of that hidden cavern that festered in the quiet moments before sleep claimed me. The horrors, meticulously documented in that tattered journal, lingering like spectres around my soon-to-be cold corpse. And yet, there's a peculiar warmth to these ghosts; they whisper not of defeat but of uprising. The journal gave me hope, and the brothers hadn't found it yet. It wouldn't be long before they did. I had to stay awake until they locked me in my room, so I could hide it somewhere… presuming I could get my damn body to move more than an inch at a time!

Xander stopped and I could see Edison's boots, as he stepped closer to me. I shuddered inside, recalling a memory so strong it burnt a hole in my mind, branding my body with his stench. A memory carved into my mind like a stain you just can't remove. It leeches there, unwrapping itself when I dream, startling me awake; and it's always plagued me ever since, every time I looked in the mirror, every time I feel his scars. But these scars were more than what you could see on the outside. These ran deep. The coward had not only taken me as his, but he had also written the word 'mine' with his blade, as two of his friends held me down.

It started at a party. His party, one which he said he held in my honour. You see Edison had found out it was to be my fourteenth birthday when he overheard the girls and I talking about celebrating in our bedroom together. We always tried to make a fuss on any occasion like that. It was something to look forward to, and Natasha said, any sweet fourteen-year-old deserved a party. I remember smiling until the door creaked open and Edison stood there grinning.

"How about I through you a party Babydoll," he said. His face was sinister and mischievous.

I shuddered but did not reply. I knew better to speak unless spoken to, and what he asked, was not a question.

"Tonight. Be ready at eight, you will be our guest… and girls, you will serve." Natasha, Jess and Beth nodded. I bit my lip and feigned a smile, hating my life somewhat more at that moment. After Edison left I ran and sat on my bed, fearful of what tonight would mean. Edison never did anything nice. Everything always had an ulterior motive.

"It will be okay," Jess said, stroking my hair. "Maybe he wants to throw a nice party."

I looked at her wide-eyed. "Remember the last party?" I bit back. She gulped. The last one ended with Beth a mess of tears in the corner, Natasha black and blue and Jess and I tied to bedposts all evening. It was disgusting. I hated my life.

Xander carried my limp body through the rest of the labyrinth of tunnels, out into the mansion, and then threw me down on the bed. "She's out of it," he said.

"What about the others?" Edison asked.

"They're caged and ready to go." He nodded.

Stefan walked over and prodded me. "She needs to come too. She can't stay here anymore. Not after what they all did to Uncle."

Edison growled under his breath and punched me in the stomach in anger. I coughed and spluttered, curling up into a ball, tears rolling down my eyes. Some movement had come back, but my eyesight was still blurry and the room still span.

"Fine. Get her in the car. She can go to. But you're explaining to him."

Xander grabbed me again, flung me over his shoulder and walked out of the room. "Xander, grab a change of clothes for them all, they will need them," Edison yelled as he left.

"Fucks sake."

We walked back into the room as he pulled apart the drawers, grabbed a handful of nightdresses and headed outside toward the car.

The vibration of the car journey was lulling me to sleep, pulling me back into the memory of the night of the party.

I remember when we entered the room. A smoky haze blurred the outlines of men as they clustered like vultures in the shadows, their silhouettes warped by the dim, flickering light from the overhead bulbs. The room reeked of cigars that burned into the night, cigarettes that smouldered endlessly, and alcohol that spilt and stained the soul. I coughed—an instinctual response to the suffocating air charged with expectation.

"Get the drinks," one of the Payne brothers hissed at Natasha, shoving her toward their bar area. I glanced down at my bare arms, the chill of vulnerability tracing my spine. Clad only in my plain white underwear, the fabric might as well be translucent—offering no shield against the stares that stripped away the remnants of my dignity.

Edison grabbed my arm, pulling me forward into the middle of the leering crowd of men. "This, men, is the birthday girl!" The men burst into cheers. Edison let go of my arm and ordered Jess to crank up the volume.

Stuck in the middle of a group of drunken businessmen, I didn't know what to do. Edison stood, leaning against the wall, smirking as he watched me.

The air clung to me, humid and laced with the stench of spirits—both the liquid kind and those conjured by my frantic imagination. My skin prickled under the weight of hungry eyes, but I forced myself to stand there bare, only my bra and panties covering me.

"Come here girl," an old fifty-something man said as he pulled me over to a seating area. With each step, the floorboards groan beneath my feet, as if sharing in my trepidation. "Sit with me."

I bit my lip, remaining unspoken.

"What's your name princess?"

"Evie," I said, almost whispering.

He laughed. "My daughter's name is Evie! That won't do! I'll call you princess." Of course, you will. Every fucker seems to want to call me some made-up name.

Edison walked over, licking his lips. A move I only saw him make when he was on the prowl, and I knew what that meant. "Well, it looks like you've met our birthday girl."

"Oh I have, but she doesn't seem to want to sit too close," he said, then whole-heartedly laughed.

"Can you blame her old man!" Edison said, sitting beside me. "Come on, shift your weight. This girl's mine."

He grumbled under his breath then shuffled to the edge of the sofa, and pushed himself up once, twice, then third times a charm; finally walking away.

"Well Babydoll, it's me and you now." I shuddered, and two other men walked over.

"Are you having a party over here man?" One of them said.

Edison smirked, "Nothing you can't join in with." The newcomers laughed. My heart raced, pounding like a train threatening to derail from its tracks. Palms sweaty, brow beading with sweat. Where was this going? What were they going to do to me?

"Come on Babydoll, stand up and dance for us." I almost vomited in my mouth. I didn't know how to dance, and the last thing I wanted was to turn them on in any way.

Edison pushed me up off of the sofa. "Now," he demanded. By now a few more of the lecherous men had crowded around and the music changed to something more sensual. I stood there unable to move. "Oh, my sweet girl. Did I never teach you to dance?" He laughed and stood up, grabbing my hips and pulling me up against his body so I could feel his erection through his jeans. "That's for you Babydoll," he smirked, wrapping his arms around me, swaying my hips with his, as we slow danced.

I felt like an unwilling performer on a stage set for wolves, commanded to dance in the den of the lecherous and cruel.

One foot moving after the other, we swirled in circles and I almost found myself smiling as he glided me around the room. Edison was enjoying this, enjoying showing me he had a human side. We moved through the fog of smoke and sin, every fibre of my being screamed in protest, trying to bring me back to the reality of the situation. But somehow I lost myself there in his arms for a mere moment; aroused by his touch, swayed by his movements as he stole my first dance from me.

But as the song came to an end, the dance slowed to a darker corner of the room. I sensed the shift before it happened. Edison grinned. A roughened hand came from behind, calloused and unyielding, fastening around my arm, yanking me from Edison's arms. He laughed.

"Here now, don't be shy," the man growled spinning me around, his voice a gravelly command that drowned out the din of the room.

I came face-to-face with danger, the heat of his breath mingling with the toxic fumes of alcohol. His eyes were bottomless pits, devoid of empathy, drilling into mine with an intensity that sought to devour. For a moment, it's as if we're the only two beings in existence—predator and prey locked in a timeless dance.

I retreated, the phantom touch burning on my flesh as I banged into Edison.

"What's the matter Babydoll?" Edison said. "Don't you want to play with my friends?"

My eyes widened.

Two pairs of arms coil around mine with the certainty of pythons. Their squeeze was inescapable, fingers digging into my flesh like steel traps. I pulled away, a futile attempt to wrench myself free, but their hold was unyielding, an anchor dragging me down into depths unknown.

"Let me go," I hissed, my voice a venomous whisper that betrayed the storm of panic within.

"Easy there," one murmured, his breath a fetid gust against my neck, a stark contrast to the sterile chill that had taken root in my bones. His words were soaked in mock concern, yet they offered no comfort, only a prelude to dread.

The world tilted, and I was suddenly wrenched sideways, forced face down onto the table.

My cheek pressed against the wood, the grain rough and indifferent. Hands, more than I could count, pressed down upon me, a grotesque blanket of restraint. Their touch was invasive. My skin recoiled, every nerve ending alight with revulsion.

"Stay still darling," another voice cooed, a sibilant threat veiled in false tenderness. I could feel the heat of his body hovering over mine, a dark shadow cast by a sunless sky.

I wanted to fight, to claw and bite and break away, but their mass was a mountain upon my back, immovable and eternal. Instead, I closed my eyes, shutting out the sight of them, willing myself to become stone, to endure what must be endured.

"Please," I whisper, the plea was lost amidst

their laughter and the hammering of my heart. The word dangled in the void, unanswered, a lone cry swallowed by the night.

Pain splintered through me, sharp and relentless. The room began to spin, a carousel of shadows and half-caught leers, each twist a fresh wave of torment. With every touch, my skin crawled, revulsion thick in my throat like bile.

"Quiet now," one of them grunted, his voice a guttural rasp. His words were meant to soothe but they sliced through me, leaving invisible scars upon my mind.

I retreated within myself, away from the coarse hands that explore without permission, away from the crushing weight that stole my breath. My thoughts spiralled, desperately seeking refuge. I remember finding it in the warm embrace of a memory, a lifeline thrown across the chasm of my despair.

"Red Riding Hood didn't give up, did she, Evie?" My mother's voice was a soft melody, her face alight with the glow of the bedtime lamp. Her auburn hair cascaded around her shoulders, a fiery shield against the encroaching darkness of my bedroom.

"Never, Mama," I whispered back to her, my voice steady despite the tempest raging around me. "She was brave."

"Exactly, my love," my father added, his eyes sparkling with pride. "Just like you. Brave and clever."

I clutched the memory close, a talisman forged from the fires of innocence and love. Red Riding Hood, the girl who outsmarted the wolf, faced fear and emerged victorious. She was strong. She was determined. She was the flame that refused to be extinguished, even by the foulest of breaths.

The final echoes of their laughter splintered the silence as they withdrew, leaving me crumpled on the splintered wood, a discarded rag doll in a room that reeked of brutality. My skin crawled with the residue of their touch, a violation more profound than the physical wounds that marred my flesh.

I shuddered thinking about it. For any story, for any trauma that should be the end of it. But not for me. As a fourteenth birthday present, Edison flipped me over, took out his switchblade and carved the word MINE into my thigh, so I would have a physical reminder of that night.

"Now you know who you belong to Babydoll. Never forget that." He left me there trembling, blood running down my leg as I fell off the table, and scurried to the dark corner of the room. Natasha found me and covered me in a blanket she'd found and helped me leave the party. By then the men were too drunk to even notice us leaving.

Somewhere deep inside, something vital broke that night, the pieces sharp and glittering like shards of a shattered mirror. But within those fragments, there shone a reflection—a glimmer of who I knew I had to become. The innocence that once painted my world in soft hues had to go, replaced by the stark contrast of shadow and light, predator and prey.

I felt down to the scar and traced out the letters. Nearly two years later it was still raised on my thigh, and as I did, the brothers stopped talking, the car slowed to a stop and the door opened as Xander pulled me out and flung me over his shoulder once again.

ANNALEE ADAMS - WOLF

9

I awoke to an immense jolt of pain in the stomach. Edison's large hands, once dismissive in their touches, now clenched into fists at his sides. They are weapons, cocked and loaded, fueled by betrayal. He turned to me, the fire in his eyes leaping out, branding me as the target of his fury. He didn't say a word; he didn't need to. The crack of his fist against my ribs was deafening, a crescendo of pain that wrapped around me, squeezing the breath from my lungs. I crumpled in the chair I was bound to, feeling the bones give way beneath the pressure of his wrath.

Spittle foamed at his mouth as Stefan pulled

him back. "I want her to remember my mark," he yelled.

"She will brother," Stefan says, placing his hand on his shoulder. "But preserve her for now, or she will be worth nothing."

I couldn't help but spit out blood onto the floor. Raising my head slightly as saliva dribbled down. I groaned, wincing in pain at every movement. Taking a brief look around, it looked like I was in a basement. The windows were small and rectangular, up high and at the top of each wall. Sunlight blared through the openings giving birth to haunting shadows that loomed over me, threatening to carry me away with them into the darkness. The room itself was full of old taped-up cardboard boxes, and I was sitting on a chair in the middle of it.

Edison growled as he watched me regaining my composure. He kicked over the chair I was tied to and punched a wall. My head hit the concrete floor when I landed, blood pooling beneath me. "Damn it, man," Stefan said, picking me up, and inspecting my face. "Look what you've done."

"If you can't sell her, then we kill her," Edison snarled, still angered at my betrayal.

"You know father would never forgive us."

"I don't give a flying fuck what he thinks," he growled.

Stefan grabbed a dirty towel and pressed it against the gash in the side of my skull. Dazed and confused at where I was I could hear the cries of the others, muffled and distant. Xander must be dishing out their punishment. I just hope they survive this. Edison looked at me again and growled.

"You were mine!" He yelled, coming at me again. Stefan jumped in. "She can't take anymore Edison, you'll kill her."

"She should die by my hand than live without me." If I wasn't so messed up right now I would have thought him an arrogant prick for that comment. But I daren't move, let alone look up at him.

Although, even as he beat me, there was a method to his madness—he preserved my face, a mask of marketable innocence that he so values.

As I lay broken, his shadow loomed above, and an eerie calm began to settle upon him. "You think you've won," he sneered, spitting out the words, his voice cold and as unyielding as steel. "But you've only secured your place on the auction block."

My mind reeled from the pain, but it latched onto his words, the implication chilling me to the core. Auctioned—like cattle, like a piece of meat devoid of any purpose beyond the whims of satisfying the hunger of its buyer.

"Get her cleaned up," Edison commanded, his voice slicing the air like a knife. Stefan nodded, wary of his brother, but his shoulder slunk back down as Edison left the room.

And with that decree, Stefan untied me and

yanked me from the chair, my body protesting. Dragging me, I cried, cradling my ribs as if my organs would fall out if I didn't hold them in place. The pain was immense, as though someone had placed a red-hot poker against my skin.

Leaving the storage room, he pulled me along. "In there," he ordered. "Shower and change." I looked at him. "NOW!" My eyes widened and I hobbled in, doing as he told me.

The shower room was a grubby little bathroom, with chipped old white tiles, limescale building up over the base of the taps and the shower hose itself felt slimy to the touch. I would have gagged but held my breath to prevent myself, fearing the pain if I did. The water though, was hot, not scolding, but burning hot. Hot enough and loud enough to escape in. Beads ran over my bloodied skin, my blood mixed with their uncles, cleansing the past away, and I allowed myself five minutes to break down and cry, no matter the pain it caused my ribs to whole-heartedly sob.

At that moment I was scared. Truly. I feared the thought of what lay behind that door. I worried about where the girls were and whether they were still alive. The auction itself drove terror into my soul, what would it mean? Were we going to be separated? What would be sold into, and for what? To do, what? Sometimes the Devil you know is better than the Devil you don't. I now understood that saying, although if my life continued this way, perhaps I should have called it quits as Laney did. Maybe she had the right idea after all.

BANG BANG BANG… "Get out here Babydoll," Edison yelled and I winced at the sound of anger coating his voice.

"She's almost ready," Stefan said. "Give her two more minutes.

"What? Why?" Edison snarled. "I wouldn't want her to miss all the fun, now would I!" I could almost hear him grin through the doorway.

"Put this on her and bring her out."

After I was sure the asshole had left, I towel-dried, brushed my teeth with my finger and ran my fingers through my hair to tease it back to some kind of normality. The wound on my head had stopped bleeding and was a mere one-inch cut.

Adorning my nightdress, I slowly opened the door. "He's gone," Stefan said, as I peered out. "Wear this." He handed me a black blindfold, a significant contrast against the pure white nightdress they had made me wear. I placed it over my eyes, and Stefan tied it, ensuring it was tight and I couldn't see.

"Take my arm," he directed. I did as I was told, stepping where he told me, turning when he said until eventually, we came to a stop. Before he took my blindfold off I could smell bleach. Where the heck were we?

"Now I want you to sit down there, count down from ten, then take off your blindfold. Do you understand?"

"Yes," I replied, sitting down on the cold floor. It felt like stone, maybe concrete the same as the room I was previously in.

I heard muffled voices as I began to count down from ten. Edison's snarls and sinister laughter weren't hard to miss. But what disturbed me the most was the gurgling, sloshing sound. Like someone was wringing out a dishcloth nearby. But the gurgling, that was from a person. But who. Five, four, three, two, and one. I slowly took off my blindfold, and when I did the horror I saw before me made me want to put it straight back on again.

I was sat in a gilded birdcage, built of wrought iron, each bar mere inches from the other. In the cage lay nothing but myself, my fear, my desperation sweating from my pores, crying out for salvation. But most of all, exceeding all of that was my anger. Rage built up over the years of molestation. Fits of boiling, bubbling pain, ready to burst and take down the whole building with it.

Looking up I could see the bars coming together to form the top of the cage. It reminded me of one of the old-fashioned ones my Grandmother used to have for her pet Cockatiel Tony. I laughed inside remembering how she would repeat his name over and over, saying who's a pretty boy then. She was as loopy as a fruit cake that one. But she was the best of us. Beyond the cage lay darkness, darkness framed by steel beams. Beams that held the building up, a cage within a cage. It appeared as though I was in some kind of large warehouse.

The cement floor iced my thighs as I didn't dare to move from the spot he'd told me to sit in. But, I couldn't ignore the sloshing sound. I couldn't forget about the gurgling or the broken breaths as someone gasped for air. There was no way the memory of someone trying to scream out with no succession would ever leave my mind or this place. Her screams would remain inked into the walls, a snapshot in time, just as her blood soaked into the cement floor below her.

I knew who it was before I dared look in her direction. The youngest of us. Beth.

Taking a deep breath I looked over. My mind fastened on the face of Natasha hurling abuse through her birdcage across from my own. To the left of me, Jess held the bars and screamed until she was blue in the face, and to the right was an empty cage. One where Beth should have been, but no longer was.

"Leave her alone!" Natasha screamed. Her hair was sodden with sweat, her face broken by the tears she must have cried.

"NOOOOO…" Jess cried, covering her eyes, as the sloshing sound made Beth gurgle some more.

But still, I hadn't dared look directly down on the floor where the brothers and Beth were. Instead, I saw a bright crimson trail of blood flowing downhill toward me. I was at the base of the circle of cages, granted only downhill by a small amount, but enough to cause a flow of bodily fluids to trickle their way into my cage and down to my feet. I peered down, watching as her blood was broken by my body, like a damn in an overflowing river. Except this was no river, nor any dam. This was two people. Me, now covered in blood as I sat in it, and Beth who donated it to the cause, her gurgling lessening as we speak.

Gulping I had to move, fearing I would be overtaken by her spirit. I looked around, in hopes of any way of getting out of here. Any chance of leaving, helping Beth and releasing the others. Then gutting the brothers like the pigs they are. But there was nothing. No-one.

I pulled myself up, wobbling on two feet like a toddler taking its first steps. Edison did a number on me. That knock to the head must have been more than a cut to the head.

Putting my arms out I steadied myself, squinting to gain focus as the room began to spin like a merry-go-round. To anyone else I must have looked like a drunk person, swaying back and forth, trying to gain my balance, not daring to move for fear I'd fall flat on my face. It was too soon. Vertigo had claimed me and postural hypotension was taking me down. I slowly lowered myself on all fours, going back to basics and crawling forward, slipping and sliding through Beth's blood.

Blinking a few times, the bars soon came back into focus, and everything started feeling almost normal again. Whatever was messing with my blood pressure, or well whatever had happened when Edison tore into me, was beginning to simmer down. It was a good sign. I needed my wits about me if I had any chance of getting out of this shitty situation.

Reaching the bars, I pulled myself up. Stood for a few seconds, ignored the dizziness but held on for dear life. Taking a deep breath, I finally started to come back to reality. A reality where three brothers were pulling apart the young girl we knew and loved right before our eyes. Because there, in the centre of the bird cages, on the floor was Stefan watching as Edison punched the life out of Beth. Slamming his iron fists into her fragile, porcelain face, shattering the beauty she once treasured. Split lips, broken nose, black eyes. She looked swollen and sore. He laughed, mocking her as she cried.

"Did that hurt Sweetpea?"

She cried some more.

"What was that? You want some more?" He grinned, kicking her in the ribs.

"Hey!" Xander shouted, pushing him back. "I'm working here!" Edison laughed and sat down beside Beth, stroking her swollen face.

I looked over to see what Xander was doing, but his body covered her abdomen, so I couldn't quite see. But whatever it was made her squirm and fight with what little might she had left. It was also the culprit of the sloshing noise.

"Finished yet?" Edison said, watching him.

"Not quite!" Xander replied. The next thing I know his arm raised as he held a huge needle and thread. It reminded me of a large leather needle with a big bulky thread.

"That does look beautiful," Xander remarked at his creation.

"Ah, it's not finished yet!" Edison said while stroking Beth's swollen face. He pulled out his switchblade and began to cut around her ear, and her cheekbone, following it along over her jawbone, and all the way around until he met the other side. Beth choked and coughed, crying, trying to scream. But even Stefan was made to come and hold her down while Edison finished the cut. He almost vomited when he looked down at whatever Xander had been doing.

I stood in pure shock. Jess's screams were continuous, and Natasha joined me in shock as we stood there heartbroken for the pain our younger sister must be in right now. If only we could reach out and take her away from it all. Tears fled down my face. Weeping uncontrollably I watched as Edison edged around her eyes, then proceeded to pull her pretty swollen face away from its muscular mass below.

I slunk down to my knees, vomiting all over myself as he pulled her face away, laughing and joking, throwing it to Xander. By now my knuckles were white from gripping the bars so tight, I no longer had any feeling left in my fingers.

Beth coughed out more blood, her skull turning towards me, her eyes begging for release, praying for the pain to be over with. But instead, Xander had other ideas. Out came the large needle and thread and he continued working. I wanted to see, but at the same time, I didn't. Xander had taken Beth's childlike face, a face full of innocence and purity, a body taken too young, abused, raped and beaten over the years. She never deserved any of this, and to be treated how she was being treated now. To be disfigured in this way. I vomited again.

"And…. I'm done!" Xander remarked, pulling up the needle and tossing it to the side. Edison stood up and walked around to stand behind him, his back facing me.

"Oh, Xander. This is some of your finest work."

"Stefan come look!" A hopeful Xander said.

Stefan shook his head. "What? Why?" he whined.

"You two make me sick," he said. "Why not just kill them and be done with it? This mutilation is disturbing."

"But it's art, Stefan!" Xander said. "We could sell her at the auction. I think she would fetch a pretty price."

Edison laughed. "I wouldn't say pretty anymore, Xander. But yes. She is what you would call a living piece of art."

"See!" Xander remarked. Stefan huffed and

walked away. Xander stood up and ran after him.

"But brother!" he said, following him out of the warehouse.

Now that Xander had moved, it was only Edison's bulky body blocking poor Beth from me. I was amazed she was still alive, especially considering the amount of pain she must have just endured.

Edison turned around looking at Natasha and Jess as they sobbed in their cages. He looked at me as I sat in a heap on the floor, holding the bars like my life depended on it, while covered in Beth's blood and my vomit. He smirked.

"Want to see Babydoll?" I looked at him, wide-eyed and still in shock as Beth still faced me gurgling, spitting out blood.

"Do you want to see what killing my uncle has caused Babydoll?" He growled. He bent down and lifted poor Beth up, her fragile body now motionless to his touch, whereas once she would have recoiled.

Turning he held her higher than me. Blood dribbled down from her, pooling beneath her. I spotted that they had attached a tube, an IV of clear fluid. Shit. Was that to keep her alive? Did they purposely want her to live long enough to feel the pain they dealt her? I swallowed back bile.

Edison bent down, bringing the limp Beth with him. But as he dropped her on the floor, her broken body fell under the light by my gilded cage, and what I saw will scar me for every day I live, and forever more.

Beth's pure, perfect body had been sliced open from collarbone to public bone. Her skin had been pulled back, uncovering the muscles and ligaments that held her breasts in place. Her wrists had been broken and shattered hands stitched in place. One hand cupped each breast. Beneath it Xander had pulled out a coil of intestines, swirling it around in a spiral.

"Do you like her new body? "Edison said. I stared in shock, speechless.

"What about her face?" he asked. I looked above her swirled nest of intestines and right there, sat above was Beth's skinned face with lips stitched together and a severed finger placed over them, as she looked out at the world from inside her ribcage.

ANNALEE ADAMS - WOLF

10

After a night of pure terror, wondering if I would be the next victim of Xander's trashy art show, I had barely slept. I awoke with a start, still holding the hand of my beloved Beth. Edison had left her now rotting corpse outside of my cage, staring out me from the bloodied mess that was once her face. But at least she had not died alone. I was there with her, soothing her sorrows as she succumbed to the blood loss and pain. I will always remember her last breath, a jagged one, as though she wanted to breathe deeper but no longer had the energy to force her lungs to work any more.

Beth had been so brave. She was a fighter and hung on for as long as she could, but I told her there was no need to. Her body was ravaged, she was dying, and all she lived for now was a painful death. It was better to let go sooner than later. She didn't listen though. I half-smiled, staring at her with tears in my eyes. She was as stubborn as the rest of us.

"WAKEY WAKEY" Xander yelled, storming into the room. I jumped, dropped Beth's hand and edged to the other side of the gilded cage. He laughed when he saw me.

"Oh, Babydoll. You look all bloody! That won't do!" He smirked, walking over and kicking Beth away from the cage door, unlocking it. My heart dropped as her limp body rolled to the side.

He flung the cage door open, leaving the keys in the lock, stepped inside and remarked on the amount of blood all over the floor. As he was busy being mesmerised by the blood, I took my chance to hobble around him and limp out of the cage, slamming the door and locking it. The noise made him look up, bringing him out of the bloodlust trance he appeared to be in.

"What the hell!" He ran at the door, but by slamming it, the latch had clicked back into place. "Open this goddamn door now Babydoll or you'll be my next creation on the floor out there."

I shuddered and backed away. By now Natasha was yelling for me to open her cage. I ran over and oh my god there must have been thirty keys on this bloody thing! Shaking my head I looked around, hoping the noise hadn't alerted Edison and Stefan. But the door was closed, I was in luck… for once! What I hadn't counted on though was Xander having a mobile phone!

"Pick up! Pick up, you bastard!" he yelled.

"Shit! Hurry!" Natasha cried.

"I'm trying!"

"Give them here!" She snatched the keys. Which she was right to. My luck with keys was rather on the crappy side. She stood for a minute, staring at the lock, staring at the keys, then picked one, finding the key on her first try.

"Hurry!" Jess yelled, from the side of us. "I heard a car outside."

"Oh my god, someone must be here!"

Turning I could see Xander angrily talking on his phone, staring at the door. Damn it! They're already here!

Natasha slammed the key in the lock, and it worked the first time, opening her cage door. I half-sighed with relief as I heard the sound of squealing tyres right outside the building. That's them!

Natasha kept hold of the same key, ran over to Jess's cage, and used it on her door. What do you know, it bloody worked!

Too late though, as in this vast space, filled with nothing but our gilded bird cages, the body of our beloved sister-in-arms Beth, the corrupt and evil Xander and one getaway door, there were now two further entities that used up part of the atmosphere, Edison and Stefan. Edison was clapping, whereas Stefan was almost in tears laughing at Xander.

"Well done girls!" he said. "Had we been gone for much longer you may have tasted your freedom. But now, well, you never will," he remarked, smirking. "Instead, you three will be our prime pieces at the auction, isn't that marvellous." He walked over. "Especially you Babydoll. And I know, that you need to shower and change for the big event, so I'm going to leave you in Stefan's capable hands, for if I allowed Xander anywhere near you, I fear he may actually remove your head with his teeth." My eyes widened.

Stefan took the keys from Natasha's shaking hand and ushered the three of us out of the warehouse before Edison released Xander, who was quite literally foaming at the mouth with anger.

***

After washing and changing, we had a little food and heard Xander arguing with Edison outside the room. He was not allowed in to see us until the big event. Which I for one was relieved about. The thought of what the big event was though, well it made me shudder.

"It's time," Stefan said, looking up from his phone.

I gulped.

Jess took my hand, and Natasha's. "We've got each other," she said. "Whatever happens, none of us will be alone."

I nodded, swallowing back the tears at the thought of losing either of them, they had been my family here, just as Beth had. I couldn't lose anyone else. I couldn't survive that.

The door creaked open, slicing through our fragile moment of solidarity. We rose together as one. There was no turning back now. Whatever awaited us beyond the threshold, we would face it together.

"Stay close," I whispered, stepping forward. My body screamed in protest, but I ignored it. Pain is nothing compared to the terror of being torn away from these girls, my sisters-in-arms.

Further down the corridor, we turned to the left, then right, coming up to the vast space where our gilded cages once stood. And where Beth tragically lost her life at the hands of the monstrous Payne brothers.

The heavy door swung open with a groan. Dim bulbs dangled from the ceiling, casting sickly pools of light on the floor. What was once a vast space had changed completely. There was now a stage, which loomed at the front, a platform for our misery, bathed in a harsh spotlight that seemed designed to strip away any remnants of dignity.

Before the stage stood the predators, huddled in packs leering at other girls that were stood tied up beside the stage. How did they get there? Where were they from? I didn't know of any other girls the Payne brothers had. Natasha and Jess looked at me and I shrugged.

"Keep your head down," I murmured to them, not wanting to stand out. Jess nodded, but her eyes were wide with fear, whereas Natasha turned away and stared back at the frightened girls huddled in the corner. There were girls as young as eight, maybe nine there. I'd never seen the Payne brothers take them that young before. I pursed my lips. Maybe there's another kidnapper here too.

Stefan ushered us toward the holding area beside the other girls, and my gaze flickered over the crowd, assessing, calculating. It looked like there was an exit at the back, but it was guarded and too far away. I took a deep breath, searching for other options. There was a window high above… I sighed. That was unreachable. The options were grim; each one was a gamble against impossible odds.

I could almost taste the tension in the air,

thick and suffocating, as the auctioneer stepped up to his podium. His practised smile was a gash in the dimness, and his voice, when he spoke, had a deep reverberation that somehow managed to fill the space, commanding attention.

The faces of the buyers blurred together. I felt like nothing more than a commodity, a piece of merchandise to be bought and sold, my worth reduced to a price tag. The room was filled with an eerie silence, broken only by the sound of the auctioneer's gavel as it slammed down on the table.

"Let's begin," he announced, and a cold shiver ran down my spine. Girls from all over the city were brought together. This seemed to be the black market for slaves, organs, sex, whatever you wanted and those men out there could purchase it.

My mind raced, and my heart hammered against my ribcage like a prisoner pounding on the walls of their cell.

"Evie?" Jess's whisper was barely audible over the buzz of the crowd. Her hand found mine, a lifeline amid the storm of panic.

I nodded, squeezing her fingers. She didn't need to say anything. I knew how she felt.

The possibility of escape was a fragile thing, but we had to try. It sparked within me a desperate kind of hope. As the first girl was led onto the stage, I could feel it—not just the terror, but the fierce need to fight, to cling to every shred of who we were in the face of the abyss.

I tried to focus on anything but the fear building inside me. But the faces of those who want to own me are etched into my mind, their malicious smiles and lecherous eyes haunting my every thought.

I clung to the memories of my family, desperately trying to find strength in their love and support. Their faces flashed before my eyes: Mum's warm smile, Dad's strong embrace. I could almost feel their hands on my shoulders, steadying me, and giving me courage. But the reality of this situation was too much to bear. I was nothing more than a commodity here, a piece of merchandise to be bought and sold, my worth reduced to a price tag.

One by one, we were presented, pulled by the ropes that bound us. Natasha is forced out next. She pulls away from Edison, but all he does is laugh at her. "I'll be glad to see the back of you three," he says, yanking the ropes and dragging her onto the stage. When she walks up he passes her over to Xander, who relishes in stripping her bare for all to see.

The bids come in fast and furious, numbers that put a price on flesh and bone, on stolen innocence.

The bidders are a grotesque pack built solely through greed and lust. Their smiles twist into lecherous grins, exposing the darkness within. Eyes roam over the girls hungrily, as if they could already taste their victory, already savour the control they'll wield. There's no trace of empathy in those stares, only the cold calculation of predators assessing their prey.

"Five hundred!" a bidder calls out, his voice slicing through the chaos, setting off another round of bidding.

"Six hundred!" another counters, his tone dripping with smugness.

And so it continues, each bid a hammer striking at the ropes that bind us, each number a measure of how cheaply our lives are held. With every moment that ticks by, I feel the walls closing in, but inside, a fierce resolve simmers—a refusal to be broken, to be sold into oblivion.

"Seven hundred!"

I stand rigid, my resolve hardening like steel tempered in fire. My eyes dart around, seizing every shadow, every flicker of movement—a door left ajar, a window too high to reach, the bulky figures of guards lining the periphery. The possibilities are slim, but they are there, whispering promises of freedom.

My fists clench at my sides, nails digging crescents into my palms. I feel the heat behind my eyes, not of tears—no, those have long since dried—but of a burning rage, an inferno stoked by each degrading bid thrown carelessly into the air.

"Eight hundred!" A new bidder joins the fray, his voice laced with anticipation as if we are nothing more than trinkets to be bartered over.

"Do we have nine hundred?" the auctioneer asks the pitch of his voice climbing, slicing through the thickening atmosphere. A murmur ripples through the crowd, a wave of excitement at the prospect of owning one of us as if we're rare collectables instead of shattered souls desperate for salvation.

I can hear my heart thundering in my chest, a frantic drumbeat echoing the rising bids. Each throb is a reminder of what's at stake, of the ropes waiting to bind us even further into this nightmare.

"Nine hundred!" An eager wolf shouts out, jumping from foot to foot.

Amid the chaos, my mind races. Every strategy, every potential path to escape unfolding before me like a map written in the language of survival. I weigh the risks and the chance of failure against the slim hope of success. Yet as the bids climb higher, so does my determination.

"Going once! Going twice!"

The finality of the moment hovers, a guillotine ready to fall. The auctioneer's gavel is poised, his eyes scanning the crowd for any last takers.

"Sold!"

The word is a gunshot, a death knell that seals our fate. But it is not the end. It cannot be. Natasha is dragged from the stage, and Jess is yanked out of my arms, tears streaming down her pale face.

"And for our next auction, we have the

glorious golden prodigy, our very own Little Bird!" the auctioneer hypes up as part of his sales pitch.

Xander grabs Jess and pulls her body close to his, stealing a kiss from her lips. "Oh she's a feisty one," the auctioneer says as Jess pushes Xander away. Xander laughs and rips her nightdress off of her.

"Get a load of that innocent body, have you seen anything as pure as that?" he asks.

"I will start the bidding at seven hundred!"

No one bids.

"Oh come," he says. Xander pulls Jess around as she yells and slaps him when he tries to touch her down below. The crowd laugh, cheering him on.

"Seven hundred," one man in a mustard-coloured jacket shouts.

"Seven, fifty!" the man beside him shouts, and the two of them face each other and start to push and shove one another.

The auctioneer laughs. "Hey folks, let's let the money do the talking shall we? Not the fists! Now do I hear eight hundred?"

"A thousand!" A dark man shrouded in a hooded jacket yells from the corner.

"One thousand it is," the auctioneer yells. "Do I hear any advances on one thousand?" He looks around from left to right.

"Going once, going twice, sold to the man at the back." The hooded man nods, and as he does his hooded jacket swishes to the side, revealing a long curved blade that shines under the moonlight that spills through the smoke-stained windows.

"Well, well," Edison said. "Babydoll, it's your turn." I shuddered as he gripped my arm, pulling me into him. "I'm going to miss the fun we had together. But," he moved in to whisper into my ear. "Just remember, whoever buys you today, they will never own you. I made my mark on you. You were mine first, and will always be mine." I gulped, and he yanked me forcefully onto the stage. He was standing behind me and holding my arms in place so I couldn't fight or run off.

"Well looky here," the auctioneer said, looking me up and down. "It looks like we have a fiery redhead, tonight folks."

Xander walked over and grabbed my neck, choking me. His eyes were full of anger. Edison pulled me tighter from behind. "Not now Xander. We're selling her, remember." Xander growled, and ran his hand up and down my body, taking an extra-long time over my breasts.

Fear was soon overtaken by disgust, and disgust by anger. I used Edison's grip on me as an advantage and gripped my arms onto his, quickly raising both legs and kicking Xander smack bang in the dick. Edison flew backwards with me on top of him. Xander hurtled off of the stage and landed on top of the mustard-coloured jacket guy while holding his dick. So, I took my chance and jumped off the stage. The crowd applauded me, cheering me on as I ran for the exit on the other side of the room.

As I ran, every step I took only fueled the flames of my hatred, a hatred that had sunk its claws into the very marrow of my bones. The Payne brothers, purveyors of fear and pain, will come to know this hatred. They'll feel it in the quiet moments when they believe themselves safe. They will feel it when they walk in the darkness, and the shadows leap out to destroy them. For one day I will become their predator, and they will live only as my prey.

11

Chaos erupted in the room. Shattering glass, smoke, and shouting filled the air, momentarily distracting everyone from my dash for freedom.

My heart jackhammered in my chest, the pounding so deafening it drowned out the shouts and the screams of those around us. This was my chance, my only chance to escape this hellhole.

Eyes darting around the room, I spotted them - Edison and Stefan, their attention temporarily diverted as the exit door was blasted off of its hinges and an onslaught of police officers poured in. They're distracted, searching for a way out themselves.

My hands tremble as I navigate through the mass of people, trying to avoid fights, arrests, and gunshots. My body is fueled by adrenaline, giving me the energy to propel forward, weaving in and out of the ferocious crowd.

"EVIE!" I hear Natasha cry out from behind me. Stopping I turn, trying to find her in the smoke-filled chaos. "Get off me!" she cries, and I can hear her screams not far from the exit.

"Where are you?" I call out, listening for any reply, but all I hear are her cries for help. Fearing the worst I speed up, pushing and shoving past the predators that would have bought my body for less than a thousand not so long ago.

Hurrying, my pounding heart beat so fast I was surprised it still functioned.

I reached Natasha just as Edison was about to strike her. It already looked like she'd been punched and kicked a few times, as she lay in the fetal position on the floor.

Edison's fist was primed and ready to deliver

a devastating blow. In one fluid motion, I lunged forward, offering a silent prayer to any power that might be listening. Surprise registered on his face a split second too late as I connected my foot with his knee. His leg buckled underneath him, and Edison stumbled forward, crashing into Stefan, sending them both tumbling to the ground.

The sudden shift in momentum was all Natasha needed. I pulled her up and she winced, holding her ribs, but staggering to her feet. The look of relief in her eyes was short-lived as she glanced at me, fear warring across her features.

"Run!" I hissed, shoving her in the direction of the exit. "Now!"

Natasha didn't argue, fleeing as I turned to face my tormentors. Fury and adrenaline surged through my veins, transforming me into someone I didn't recognise. At that moment I was no longer the mild, meek Evie. I was a force of nature. I stood up for my family, and no wolf would take me down!

Edison scrambled to his feet, clutching his injured leg. His usually cocky demeanour was replaced by rage. "You bitch!" he spat, barreling towards me.

I dodged out of his path, adrenaline lending me the speed I didn't know I possessed. Grabbing a chair, I lifted it, wincing at the pain in my ribs, but still raised it high, and swung it with all my might, connecting with his back as he passed. He fell hard, skidding across the sticky floor.

Stefan was less easily deterred. He advanced on me, his eyes cold and calculating. There was no trace of the charming exterior he sometimes wore; all that was left was the monster I had glimpsed beneath.

"You think you can stop us?" he sneered grabbing me by my hair and yanking me close to him. "You're nothing, Babydoll. Just a pathetic, insignificant fly."

Anger flared within me, white-hot and ferocious. I headbutt him with all my might, relishing the crunch of cartilage as his nose shattered. His grip loosened just enough for me to wriggle free.

Backing away, I was now hyper-aware of my surroundings, desperate for a way out. My eyes landed on the open exit, glowing with moonlight, like a beacon of hope.

Behind me, I could hear Edison screaming for his minions to stop me, but I was already running. But just when I thought I'd made it, a man covered in tattoos barrelled into me as he pounded a police officer's face in. I tried to stop in time, but went smack bang into him, falling flat on my face and landing badly on my ankle, spraining it. Edison jumped on me, holding me down.

"Now now Babydoll, where were we?"

He gripped my neck tight, closing my airway. I kicked out, moving my body as he sat on top, trying to throw him off. Punching, slapping, scratching. Nothing worked. He didn't flinch when I cut up his face with my dirty nails. Nor did he care when I gauged out chunks of flesh on his forearm. Still, he held me there. His eyes were wide, certain, full of anger. That's when I realised. He won't let me go. He never planned to. His face would be the last face I see before I die. So I flitted my gaze to the side, straining to see what the tattoo guy was up to. Then as I saw him, I closed my eyes. His would be the last face I saw. Decorative designs swirled over his face, they were created both to disturb and inspire. His blood-splattered shirt would be the last thing I remembered, as my face turned from purple to blue, and finally, as I stopped kicking, and my arms turned too heavy to hold up, I thought… one day I'll fight back, just maybe, not today.

The afterlife was a place I never managed to reach. My mother and father were within grasp, torn away as I hurtled back to this life. Coughing and spluttering, my throat burning, chest like liquid metal. Trembling with pure exhaustion I remained unmoving, unsure why, and how I was alive, and where Edison was.

With blurred eyesight, the darkness hazed before me, lit only by moonlight as it streamed in through the broken windows. The police must have thrown in some kind of smoke grenades as I could hardly see a thing.

But as the dust settled, I found myself surrounded by the aftermath, taking a moment to catch my breath. I turned to the side to see bloodied bodies littering the floor of the warehouse.

"Oh good, you're alive!" an older male voice said with relief. I remained still, looking upward as an older gentleman in a suit approached me.

"What's your name?"

I tried to talk, but my voice was shattered, nothing came out but croaks and half-syllables.

"It's okay, save your voice. I'll call you Red.

The paramedic said you're lucky to be alive." I nodded, my neck aching as I did. He offered me a hand. "Can you stand?" his voice filled with compassion and understanding. My heart swelled with gratitude as I realised I was finally safe.

I took his outstretched hand, my trembling fingers pale against his strong grip. Shadows danced across his face, and for a moment, I'm back in the basement, trapped with no way out.

"It's alright, Red," he said, his voice calming my fractured soul. "It's over now."

The room span, and darkness edged at my vision as the older gentleman with kind eyes stood beside me, supporting me on one side. He is a refuge in this storm, a lighthouse guiding me home.

I take one last look at the auction room, the place that held me captive and the site of my Beth's murder, and vowed to never forget the horrors I endured.

The man in the suit guides me away from

the carnage, and I try to focus on the present—on the rustle of leaves under my feet, the chill in the air, and the sound of sirens, as more join the battle.

But every step we take away from the auction house is a reminder of how far I still have to go.

In my mind's eye, the faces of the girls I couldn't save haunt me, their pleading eyes a constant reminder of my failure.

I remember their beautiful, innocent faces, and I vow to make them proud. To honour their memories by living a life they were denied.

Together, we walk away from the ashes, my protector's hand warm and reassuring against my back.

We speak in hushed tones about the future, this new life that awaits me—one filled with healing and hope.

But I know the truth.

The Payne brothers may be nothing now but

memories, but the ghosts of my past will haunt me forevermore.

OTHER BOOKS BY ANNALEE

The Resurgence series:
The Heart of the Phoenix
The Rise of the Vampire King
The Fall of the Immortals
The Birth of Darkness

The Fire Wolf Prophecies:
Crimson Bride
Crimson Army

The Shop Series:
Stake Sandwich
The Devil Made Me Do It
Strawberry Daiquiri Desire

The Celestial Rose Series:
Eternal Entity
Eternal Creation
Eternal Devastation
Eternal Ending

Gruesome Fairy Tales:

Gretel

Hansel

Red

Wolf

AUTHOR'S NOTE

Thank you for reading Wolf, I hope you enjoyed the story! I always appreciate your feedback and would be grateful if you could leave me a review on Amazon– just a few words make all the difference!

As with all authors, reviews mean the world to me. It keeps me going, helps me strengthen my writing style and helps this story become a success.

CONNECT WITH ANNALEE

Join Annalee on social media. She is regularly posting videos and updates for her next books on TikTok and Facebook.

Join Annalee in her Facebook group:

Annalee Adams Bookworms & Bibliophiles.

Also, subscribe to Annalee's newsletter through her website - for free books, sales, sneak previews and much more.

Subscribe at www.AnnaleeAdams.biz

TikTok: @author_annaleeadams

Website: www.AnnaleeAdams.biz

Email: AuthorAnnaleeAdams@gmail.com

Facebook: https://www.facebook.com/authorannaleeadams/

ABOUT ANNALEE

Annalee Adams was born in Ashby de la Zouch, England. Annalee spent much of her childhood engrossed in fictional stories. Starting with teenage point horror stories and moving on up to the works of Stephen King and Dean Koontz. However, her all-time favourite book is Lewis Carroll's, Alice in Wonderland.

Annalee lives in the UK with her supportive husband, two fantastic children, little dog, and kitten. She's a lover of long walks on the beach, strong cups of tea and reading a good book by candlelight.

Printed in Great Britain
by Amazon